I0825261

IRONSHIELD'S SHADOW BOOK 1

BEGINNINGS

JB CAINE

WITH

LEA SCISM AND SAM HAMILTON

Illustrations by Grace Brooks

Cover design by Olivia Pro Design

Contents

Dedications

from JB Caine

I dedicate the writing of the IRONSHIELD stories to Lea, Sam, Jinny, Jon, Ashton, Riley, Parker, Andrew, Justin, and Cem. These characters live because of you.

My Sundays will never feel the same.

from Lea Scism

I dedicate IRONSHIELD to my beloved Speech/Debate DnD crew, for allowing me to drag them into the fantasies that once only lived in my head; to JB and Sam, for helping to make our stories flourish beyond what I ever could have imagined; and to my mom, who has always been my biggest supporter. Thank you all for everything you do.

from Sam Hamilton

I dedicate IRONSHIELD to the very first, the best, and largest D&D group I'll ever DM for. To Lea, for allowing me the honor of stepping foot in their world; and JB, for giving the story a physical form I never expected. And to Sister, who literally had to help me write this dedication and bio. I wouldn't be here without y'all.

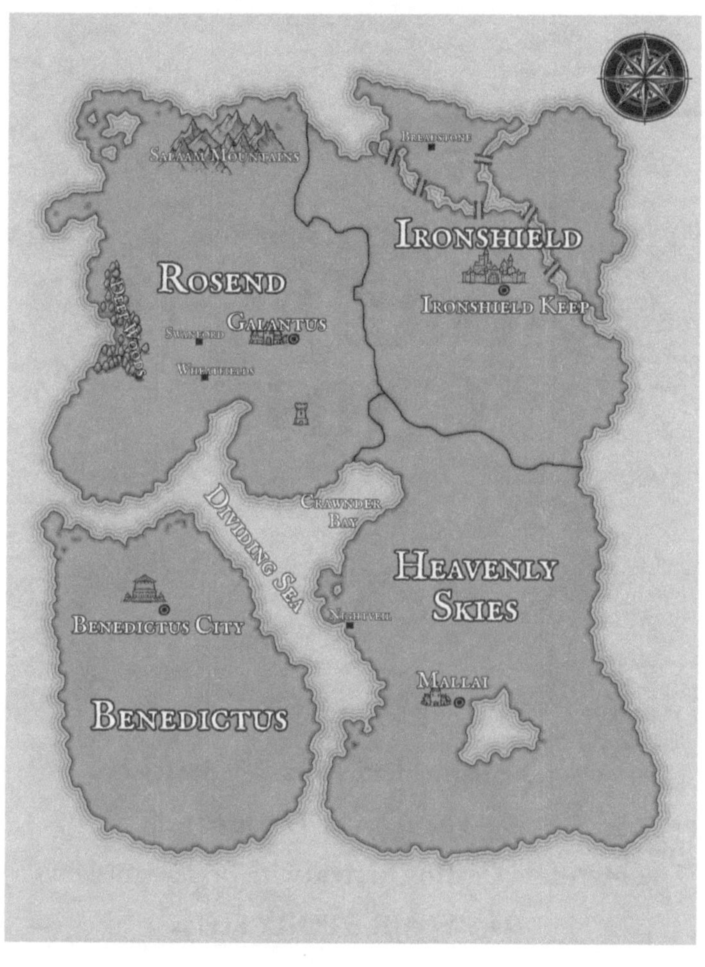
Salaam Mountains
Breadstone
Ironshield
Rosend
Deep Woods
Ironshield Keep
Galantus
Swanford
Wheatfields
Crawnder Bay
Dividing Sea
Heavenly Skies
Benedictus City
Nightveil
Mallai
Benedictus

More by JB Caine

The Ironshield's Shadow Series

The Arcana Trilogy

The Manifest Destiny Series (with Betsey Kulakowski)

The YOUR STORY Series

Chapter One

A Cast of Characters

Daijera

The Black Moon was everywhere and nowhere.

That is to say, operatives of the Black Moon were spread across the four kingdoms like pollen on a summer wind, but their influence — their very existence — was one of the world's best kept secrets.

Partly because the Black Moon paid very well.

Partly because revealing its existence was a self-imposed death sentence.

Daijera Haatengati sat in the waiting room of a posh beauty salon, carefully dressed to blend in with the upper-crust clientele while not shining brightly enough to attract undue attention. Fortunately, minor illusion magic was so common in these establishments that no one sensitive enough to notice the enchantment would think to question it.

Salons like these charged top prices for magical beauty enhancement, but Daijera's illusion was not that sort. She was lovely enough on her own, even stunning when she wanted to be. The illusion magic she cast on herself was for the purpose of light disguise ... to mask the slightly greenish tinge to her smooth skin and the slitted olive-colored serpent eyes under her dark lashes. Both were inherited from her mother, and were an ever-present reminder of the perils of standing out, even amongst the diverse population of Heavenly Skies.

There was a quiet bustling in the back room, followed by a barely audible whisper to the girl working the reception desk. She nodded in acknowledgement to the disembodied voice. "Savita will see you now," she chirped, and stepped from behind the desk to pull back a silky purple curtain.

Daijera rose and moved sinuously toward the opening. “A pleasure as always, Breta,” she smiled as she entered the back hallway that paying clientele never got to see. She moved through the dark passage toward Savita’s office and knocked carefully on the door. *Knock, knock, swish, knock.* Then she placed her hand on the handle and felt the familiar pricking of the locking spell reading her identity before clicking open and allowing her to enter.

Savita, a stately and mature elven woman, looked up as Daijera entered and smiled approvingly. “I do appreciate your prompt response to my summons,” she began, and motioned for Daijera to join her on the couch. “Have some tea, dear.”

Under ordinary circumstances, Daijera wouldn’t accept a drink from someone she didn’t know well, but this was Black Moon business, and the Code guaranteed that Savita wouldn’t have slipped poison or any other compound into her drink. Besides, Savita always had jeren-root tea, which was exceedingly difficult to find this far from the Southern Fields.

“I won’t take too much of your time, dear, because I’m going to need to dispatch you on business this very afternoon.”

"This afternoon?" Daijera raised her eyebrows in surprise. "I wasn't aware there were any missions on the calendar this week. What's the mark?"

"I do love how you always cut straight to the heart of the matter. It's part of what makes you so good at gathering information. You know just what questions to ask. Yes, indeed. And you're right, this did come up rather suddenly, and in fact, it comes from fairly high up the chain. You're needed as back-up on a very important courier mission."

"Courier? Are you sure I'm the right person for that job? I'd never undercut my own skills, but pick-up-and-delivery isn't really my area of expertise." Daijera smiled and gestured at her dancer's physique. Nice legs and long hair were very useful tools for getting people to drop their defenses and share secrets, but not particularly helpful in fighting off road bandits.

Savita chuckled. "This is no ordinary intelligence- gathering operation, dear. I'll be sending you about two days' journey to the western border of Rosend, where a wizard named Zaos Craxinna has advertised in a nearby town that he urgently needs a courier three dawns from now. Allistair dispatched two of his delivery agents to answer the advertisement, but since it was open to the public, we'd like to have another agent present who isn't already associated with the other two. If many people ... or the wrong people, rather ... answer this Zaos fellow's summons, we may have need of your *other* skillset."

"I see," Daijera nodded. *Other skillset* meant they might need someone to die a mysterious death. She dragged her tongue across the venom sac in the roof of her mouth. One more gift from mother. Viper's Breath. Very rare, and after about five minutes, completely undetectable. Assassin work wasn't Daijera's favorite thing, so she didn't generally pick up those jobs when they came available. There were plenty of operatives who were willing to take up killwork because the paycheck was about five times what smuggling, secret-brokering, or even infiltration jobs commanded. But when it came to stealth, Viper's Breath was an unparalleled weapon.

Savita pulled out a map of the Heavenly Skies/Rosend border. "Zaos has a residential tower here," She pointed to a wooded area just inside the kingdom of Rosend. You'll need to arrive at first light in three days. The other two operatives should arrive at about the same time, presumably with a passel of other people who respond to the flyer. Zaos is offering 500 crowns for successful delivery of a package to an as-yet-unspecified location."

"Wizards and their towers," Daijera sighed. "So cliché, really. But 500 crowns? What's in the package?"

"We aren't really sure, but we have intercepted some intel through the library system that this Zaos fellow has been studying some extraordinarily powerful arcane magic. If he's willing to pay that much to have something delivered, it must be something of enormous value. The three of you are to determine what the contents of that package are, and if it happens to be a particular item Black Moon is seeking, you are to find a way to get it into Allistair's hands instead of the intended destination."

"What if the item isn't the one you want?"

Savita shrugged and sipped her tea. "Then you make the delivery and collect the fee. A nice bag of gold and well worth the trip, wouldn't you say? But if it is the item we seek, then agents of King Godfroy from Ironshield also seek it. They must not get their hands on it under any circumstances."

Daijera's eyes grew wide at the mention of Ironshield's king. If Godfroy was planning something with this mystery object, then it would be a great pleasure to dispatch any of his genocidal minions who crossed her path.

"And as I said, dear, the advertisement was public. There is no telling how many fools will show up, if only for the gold."

"Ah, so I'm there in case there are too many other interested parties."

"You do catch on so quickly, dear. Yes, you do. Keep track of your activities and how many of the extra individuals you have to dispatch. You'll be well compensated when you report to Allistair. Off with you now, my dear, and here's a small down payment for your services as well as covering your passage across the Dividing Sea. It's the faster route, and you are in a bit of a hurry," Savita smiled, pulling out a small satchel of coins. She patted Daijera's knee, indicating that business had been concluded. "You'd better get going. Many miles to travel."

Dalgis

Dalgis waited patiently. He was very good at waiting.

This morning he had also waited, watching the salmon in the river as they swam around his sinewy brown legs as though he were a tree. They swam around him until, in a burst of strength and speed, he thrust his two sword-like foreclaws straight down, impaling a fish on each. He drew his arms forth and inspected his catch with satisfaction.

Splashing up to the shore to enjoy his breakfast, he lay the fish down on the rock and began the arduous process of trying to cut it into pieces with that same foreclaw. It would be much easier to gulp the fish down whole or tear them apart with the cone-like teeth that, when he wasn't eating, created a menacing grin. But that wasn't how civilized people ate, and his father and brother had always wanted him to try and be civilized. So he awkwardly cut the fish into chunks before chomping it down.

Unfortunately, his attempt at politeness also meant he ate more slowly than was natural out here in the deep forest, and the combination of the splashing sounds of his catch with the scent of fresh fish blood had attracted the attention of a very unwelcome visitor.

The bear crept toward Dalgis uncertainly, no doubt because it wasn't at all sure how much of a threat this unusual-looking beast might be. Dalgis was larger than the bear, certainly, but he was also covered in green and brown feathers with an eye-catching frill around his elongated face, and rather resembled a very fearsome looking goose. It was no wonder the bear hesitated, and that hesitation was all the time Dalgis needed.

With a roar that sounded more like a deep and resonant *honk*, Dalgis charged. The bear was still unsure what it was fighting, but it knew it had to fight or die. With a bone-crushing crunch, the two predators slammed into one another. Dalgis's girth and momentum was an enormous advantage, and as the two beasts grappled, snarled, and snapped at each other, it became quickly apparent to the bear that it was outmatched and should have sought to catch its own breakfast. Its aggression turned to fear and desperation, and it fought like a creature possessed, biting at Dalgis's arms and shoulders.

Dalgis pulled one arm back to try and run the bear through with his fearsome claw, but the bear unexpectedly thrust its neck forward and buried its teeth in the meat of Dalgis's bicep. He threw his head back and roared in pain. The bear, thinking it may have secured an advantage, clamped down harder, but that was to be its undoing. It had failed to account for the flexibility of Dalgis's long neck, and was completely unprepared when his massive maw closed around its snout and eyes. The bear tried to let go, but it was too late; the strength in Dalgis's jaws was inescapable. *Crunch* and the bear went limp, its skull split and its head crushed.

Once he was sure it was dead, Dalgis opened his mouth and let the bear fall to the ground. He looked at its body grumpily. He hated to waste a kill, but he had no taste for bear meat. Ah, well, most likely some of the forest scavengers would find the bear before too long, and it would still serve to feed other creatures. Still, he felt a twinge of regret that he hadn't been able to reason with the bear, but bears weren't people, and they didn't reason when it came to fish.

And Dalgis hadn't been about to give up his breakfast.

It was going to be a splendid day; of that he was certain. A little bit of salmon and a hearty tussle could not but bode well. *Adventure awaits you today,* said the little voice in his head. *It is the beginning of exciting things, and the path of your destiny is that much closer.* The truth was, Dalgis felt that most days were splendid. But there was something different in that feeling this morning: a feeling that today would be ... IMPORTANT. And so, after savoring his breakfast and washing off the remnants of the morning's battle, Dalgis set forth, moving quietly among the trees and parallel to the great trade road that ran from the northern ports of the Dividing Sea through the center of the Kingdom of Rosend. There were quite a few travelers today; mostly carts taking their wares to markets in the capital city of Galantus, but merchants weren't likely to lead him to his destiny, so he kept his eye out for individual travelers, particularly those who looked like they were ready for an adventure.

If he had been anyone else, he might have been discouraged after four hours of thoroughly dull people- watching. No one he had seen thus far had an aura of destiny, which was disappointing. But Dalgis never doubted what his father had called his *internal compass*. Dalgis always trusted that he was exactly where he should be, exactly when he was meant to be there.

So when he spotted the man with mottled deep brown skin, he knew his waiting was over. He moved toward the edge of the trees and waited for the man to come closer. The stranger was finely dressed in chain mail and a cream-colored cloak, with a hammered silvery breastplate glowing in the afternoon sun. He looked to have some sort of elven ancestry, but the features weren't quite a match for the other elves Dalgis had seen. When the man drew close, Dalgis extended his massive upper body out of the treeline.The knight started at the sight of the unusual beast before him, drawing his longsword so quickly that it was nearly a blur. His bushy black eyebrows rose and his eyes widened.

"Now, now, my good man, I assure you there's no need for that. Allow me to introduce myself. I am Dalgis Warclaw." As he spoke, Dalgis slowly stepped out of the trees and into the light. He drew himself up to his full height, nearly twice that of the man, and then bowed deeply. He attempted a friendly smile, but he feared that the result looked a bit more pointy and threatening than warm and welcoming. "I seek a great adventure, and my instincts tell me that with you as my companion, I shall surely find it."

The man lowered his weapon slightly, but maintained his defensive stance. "What manner of beast are you, Dalgis Warclaw? I have traveled the four kingdoms, and never have I seen anything at all like you."

"That is because there is no other like me. My father was a great sorcerer, and he fashioned me into a unique being before magically incubating and hatching me." Dalgis raised himself from his bow and stood at his most comfortable height, somewhat taller than the man but not so much so that the man would have to crane his neck to have a polite conversation. "He was a genius, my father. I miss him terribly."

"I see," said the knight, "and was he famous for his genius? Would I know his name or the story of his deeds?"

"Alas, no, my new friend. My father was executed for his genius, not celebrated. It is a great tragedy. I was very young at the time and, had I not fled Ironshield's borders, I do not doubt that I would have been killed and served to King Godfroy himself as a great feast." Dalgis's eyes grew wistful.

"Well, you do rather resemble an extraordinarily large goose, albeit one with arms instead of wings, and your legs look a bit like they belong on a young dragon. I don't wonder that Ironshield came for your father; Godfroy tries very hard to maintain only human occupants within Ironshield's borders. I can't imagine he would appreciate or condone the creation of new beasts through magic, particularly ones with the powers of speech and reason." His words were flat and practical, perhaps even a shade unkind, but the knight seemed to decide something, and sheathed his sword.

"Right you are, good sir. And one day I shall avenge my father and the impostor king will meet my claws. I will watch the light die in his eyes, just as I had to watch it die in my father's."

"You seem rather ... open ... about your past, Dalgis. Are you sure that's wise? You don't know anything about me. I might not be very trustworthy."

Dalgis grinned. "I have excellent instincts."

The knight's face broke into a smirk and he chuckled. "So you do, so you do. My name is Ren, and I would be pleased to walk with you, Dalgis. My destination is another full day's walk from here, I believe. You are welcome to accompany me. I am not sure how much adventure we will find, but I am certain that traveling with you will be anything but boring."

"Well met, Sir Ren! I shall be most honored to walk with you. I deduce that you are a man with many stories to tell, and I do love a good story. What is this destination of which you speak?"

"I travel to a wizard's tower on the southwestern border of Rosend. The wizard I seek has collected a great deal of research that, should it fall into the wrong hands, would be catastrophic. He reached out to me a fortnight ago and asked if I would consider delivering it to a library in Galantus."

"That sounds like a marvelous adventure," Dalgis replied cheerfully.

"Let's hope so," Ren smiled. "The old fool is impatient and impetuous. He asked me to arrive at dawn, two days hence. I fear that if I am delayed, he will try to transport the research himself. He's too tempting a target for highway bandits. He may be a wizard, but he's an old and addle-brained one."

"Then we make sure to arrive on time, Sir Ren! Fear not! Dalgis is with you, and you shall not fail in your task."

Ren chuckled again. "You have the heart of a knight, Dalgis."

For a moment (but ONLY a moment), Dalgis was speechless. It was the greatest compliment he had ever received.

Ekko

Attempting to remain motionless while suspended from a rafter is no small task, even if the person attempting it is, indeed, quite small. Ekko tensed all her muscles, her limbs splayed out like a flattened spider. She was close enough to the wall to press the big toe on her right foot against it, which more or less stopped her from swinging, but even in her gray tights and tunic, she wasn't sure how well she blended into the shadows of the high ceiling.

It wouldn't have been a problem if the tavern owner hadn't come back in after closing to search for the earring he had dropped at some point during the night's business. But here he was, going back and forth behind the bar with a candle, hoping to find the twisted gold hoop his wife had given him for his birthday. He was very proud of it, and talked about it incessantly to any of the bar patrons who would listen. He loved to tell the story of how his wife had secretly taken on extra mending jobs for nearly six months while he was at work so she could buy the lavish gift. Gold was rare, he said, and an industrious woman was even more so. It was that last part that had raised Ekko's ire two nights ago. Braggadocio was fine, even admirable, but levying a blanket insult against womankind in the process was foul play.

The man searched for several minutes and then finally gave up, cursing the darkness and promising himself to find the hoop in the morning when Hohn woke the sun and called it high into the sky. He kicked over a chair in frustration, then let himself back out.

Ekko let out a deep breath and let her body go limp, her muscles already twitching with exertion. Then she let loose the clamp on her belt and rolled horizontally down the semi-taut rope, landing silently on the tavern floor. She pulled a small satchel out of her backpack and crept behind the bar where were two shelves well-stocked with spirits above and beyond the cheap ale and wine most of the tavern's customers ordered. Most of the bottles on these shelves were rare, expensive, and untouched, waiting for high-class patrons to come and toast a new title, a pregnancy, or a lucrative business deal. Ekko smirked at the man's hubris. No self-respecting noble would ever make his or her way into this small tavern on the outskirts of Galantus, closer to farms and fields than it was to estates and villas. Another failing of attitude against the tavern owner. It was time he learned that there was a fine line between ambition and arrogance.

Ekko had inspected the building closely and had found a loose roof board that allowed her narrow frame to slip into the rafters above. From this perch, she had watched the proprietor close down the tavern for the last two nights, and had planned her entry and exit very carefully. Sadly, there would be no cash in the strong box because the owner had been wise enough to take any crowns with him when he went home for the night. There might still be a few coppers, but that was hardly worth the time and effort it would take to pick the lock, so she had targeted another way to ensure herself a decent payday at his expense.

Climbing nimbly on to the counter behind the bar, Ekko began removing the most ornate and expensive bottles and placing them carefully into her satchel, sliding slips of fabric between them to keep them from clinking together. The bag was not a large one, but she managed to fit eight of the bottles into it, and was still able to secure the flap. There were many places in the royal forest (a small copse of trees which created a bit of a fence between the working class and aristocratic neighborhoods of Galantus) where the young nobles gathered for their little bonfire parties, pockets full of crowns, but too young to purchase spirits. They weren't supposed to be there, but as long as they didn't cause too much trouble, the militia paid them no mind because of their parents' power and influence.

Ekko knew these bottles would fetch a pretty price with the youths, no questions asked.

She slung the bag over her head cross-body and looped her leg deftly around the rope, climbing once again into the shadows from whence she had come. She wound up the rope, slipped out through the loose roofing, and shimmied down a nearby tree. *Almost too easy*, she thought, as she sauntered down the back streets and toward the royal forest. Yes, she'd easily sell all eight bottles within the hour.

Smiling to herself, she reached into the hidden pocket in her vest and ran her thumb across a small bit of soft and twisted metal, easily nicked out of the ear of an arrogant and brusque tavern owner as he'd thrown her out for being too young to be inside the bar. Tomorrow, she thought, perhaps she'd find a nice goldsmith's apprentice who could melt it down and make her a pretty ring. Indeed, that seemed like a very good way to spend the money she was about to earn.

It took Ekko about three days to spend the money she'd earned from the sale of the liquor. She'd bought some new boots, slept in three different inns, and feasted like it was the Autumn Festival. She also had a lovely gold ring set with small red stones that glinted like blood droplets in the sunlight. She was a smart thief, though, and a smart thief knew when it was wise to blow town for a while. Besides, she wanted to hunt, and that meant heading into the woods.

She hiked into the low hills outside of Galantus and followed the setting sun to the clearing with the ancient angel oak. She loved this tree because it didn't just grow UP, it grew OUT, its lower branches arching upward, but then curving back toward the earth and stretching parallel to the horizon. She leapt onto one of its sideways branches and walked it like a beam until she reached the massive trunk. She smiled to see that the little climbing notches she'd cut into the bark were still there, and she scampered up until she found the hollow space she'd cut into the trunk at the junction of two massive branches. She laid her satchel into the hollow, then piece by piece removed her weapons and clothing, folding them meticulously, wrapping them in her short cloak and placing the cushion-shaped package into the hollow as well.

The sun was just kissing the horizon, and she stretched and felt the day's last rays on her skin. She took a deep breath and rolled her shoulders, calling to the beast within to come forth, to run, to hunt. She felt the familiar tremor begin deep in her gut and spread through her like an itchy heat. She crouched on the massive branch so she wouldn't lose balance as her bones began to morph into new shapes.

Then came the familiar tickle as the fire-colored fur burst forth and covered her new frame. Finally, there was a little popping sound as her tailbone exploded to ten times the length it was in her humanoid form. The entire transformation took less than a minute, and where a small human-looking girl had climbed into the tree, a slender and agile fox hopped down.

Ekko sniffed the air to get a sense of what she'd be chasing tonight, and she couldn't help being disappointed. She smelled boar and deer, but both of those were too big a quarry to go after. Even if she could manage to down either of those, she'd never be able to eat that much. She trotted into the forest, searching for more suitable prey, and it wasn't long before she caught the scent of a nearby rabbit warren. Her whiskers twitched in excitement. It wouldn't be long before the cottontails came out for the evening to forage. The hunt was on.

With her adrenaline flagging and her belly full of rabbit meat, Ekko made her way back to the great oak. Though she was full, she managed to leap onto the branch and walk along its length until she had returned to the hollow with all of her possessions. She stretched her vulpine limbs and nestled into the cushion of clothing she had made. Before long, she drifted off into a deep and dreamless sleep.

As dawn painted the sky, Ekko woke up and stretched, yawning so widely that her pointy little teeth were all dappled in pink sunlight. She gave a satisfied little yip, and prepared to shift back to human form and make her way into Duckwallow, a small hamlet just south of her clearing. The fiery fur receded, and the sun warmed her fair skin. She dug through her backpack, and selected a purple and crimson riding dress and breeches. She'd look significantly less thief-y, and might be able to pick up a little legitimate employment if there were a tailor or jeweler in town. If she could find some work, she could stay a little longer in town.

The problem with being a dual-natured creature is that it was difficult to remain satisfied. The part of Ekko that was fox loved stalking prey and running in the woods. She liked drinking from cool, fresh streams and the adrenaline rush of swiping unwary chickens from farms on the outskirts of town. But the part of her that was human craved civilization and the society of others. She liked festivals and music and fine clothes and comfortable beds.

She hopped down from the tree with her bags expertly re-packed, except for a small bag with five crowns in it, which she tucked safely back into the hollow of the tree. She had several of these small stashes in similar spots all over southern Rosend: some with money, some with fake documents, some with disguises, some with all three. One can never be too prepared in case one needs to leave somewhere in a hurry.

The town of Duckwallow was relatively small, with maybe 400 residents if one included the outlying farms (some of which had *marvelous* chicken coops). The sun was high in the sky as Ekko strolled up the main street. The town center had a sundial and a waterpump, as well as a small raised gazebo which was probably used for town gatherings and festivals. Gazebos like this one were fairly common, and often had a part of the base dedicated to town postings. In such places, one might find postings by townspeople looking to buy or sell a goat, notices about upcoming events, or even (Ekko hoped) announcements about businesses looking to hire a little extra help.

Today's notices were more meager than she would have liked. There was a sign offering a reward of 100 crowns for the capture or killing of a group of highway bandits (good money, but Ekko felt it would be hypocritical to take such a job), a flyer calling on followers of Epi (the Goddess of Purity) to gather together to discuss how they might better serve the town, and a job posting offering 500 crowns to deliver a very important package to a location to be disclosed at such time as someone was chosen to complete the job.

Ekko's eyes grew wide. 500 crowns was a small fortune. She could live in luxury for months with that kind of money! She reached up and snatched the announcement off the community board. It instructed her to be at a tower belonging to the wizard Zaos Craxinna at dawn, three days hence. If the package was small enough, it would be an easy job, though the high pay indicated that the wizard anticipated danger, which also probably explained why the advertisement was still there. Not many farmers would be fool enough to take such an errand, knowing it was probably deadly or illegal. Or quite possibly both. If she couldn't get the parcel to its destination, though, she could probably resell it for a decent enough price to one of the questionable merchants she knew. Pretty stupid of Zaos Craxinna to advertise this way; any manner of shady characters might answer his summons. That thought gave Ekko a chuckle. Shady characters indeed.

Chapter Two

The Quest

Sora

Blood debts sucked. And blood debts sucked even more when the person you owed the blood debt to was someone like Xezia. He always needed something, and because a blood debt was never paid in full until you either died or saved the person's life in return, you had to be essentially on-call for years at a time.

Smuggling was a dangerous business; there was no doubting that. And working for the Black Moon meant guarding the lives of near-strangers on almost every assignment. Sora had lost count of how many people she'd fought alongside while defending Black Moon cargo. It was a bit like being a soldier, only it usually wasn't legal, and it always paid well. Fighting shoulder-to-shoulder with other Moonies, as she liked to call them (in her head, never out loud ... no self-respecting smuggler would ever say something like that out loud), was part of the deal, and she'd saved many lives and had hers saved in return. Fighters were just like that, regardless of what cause they followed.

Mages, though, didn't understand or subscribe to that philosophy. So when it came to pass that Xezia saved Sora from being impaled by a spear, he pronounced a blood debt, and here she was, a year later, still following the bastard around and doing his bidding.

Fortunately, she'd come to like him, after a fashion. He was moody and serious most of the time, but it was good fun to watch him masterfully run a grift or convince people to buy them drinks and give them free lodging. He didn't even need magic to do it; he was just damned persuasive and charming when he wanted to be.

"Where are we going now, Xezia? I thought we were headed for the sea so we could make it to Benedictus by the end of the month." Sun on her right shoulder told her that they were heading north instead of west through the deep woods along the northern border of Heavenly Skies. Her copper skin shimmered in the morning light, and like all sun elves, the sun's rays fed her body and soul, made her body stronger and her mind clearer. But even the sun couldn't improve her mood.

Xezia smirked as he often did when he knew something she didn't. She hated that smirk, but it usually meant a good payday. "I got a message from Allistair last night. He's got a job for us, and it's right up your alley this time."

"And this job requires us to travel through the war zone?"

"It does. We need to get to Rosend within the next two days. But we'll veer a little to the west and avoid most of the soldier patrols. We'll have to take a short ferry across Crawnder Bay, but it will be a safer journey that way." Xezia twiddled with the obsidian holy symbol of Epi that hung on a leather strap around his neck. He always did that when he was planning.

"What do you mean it's *right up my alley*?" Sora was suspicious of anything that sounded like a favor.

"It's a courier job, you might say. We pick up a package from a wizard in Rosend and agree to deliver it to wherever he wants it delivered."

"*Agree* to deliver it?"

"Precisely. Allistair thinks it might be an artifact he seeks. If it is, we deliver it to him instead."

"This sounds far too easy," Sora observed.

"Clever as always, Sora. You're correct. There are likely to be other parties interested in serving as courier. The fee is substantial."

She gritted her teeth. "So we're expected to dispose of the competition? You know that's not how I work, Xezia, blood debt or no. I'm no assassin, and neither are you."

His smirk became a grin. "Not to worry. Allistair has that covered. He's reached out to other associates to send back-up from within Rosend. Someone who we've never met, so no connections can be made. My understanding is that this person will make contact once we've secured the package and determined its contents."

Sora nodded. She disliked assassins as a general rule, but if it kept that sort of wetwork off her hands, then she'd tolerate one. She wasn't squeamish about killing, but contract kills lacked honor somehow. It wasn't the heat of battle. It was cold-blooded and impersonal.

"What's the pay?" she asked. It was sort of an academic question. If Allistair sent orders, you couldn't exactly say no. But if the fee was *substantial*, as Xezia put it, then that provided a little incentive and motivation.

"The wizard is offering 500 crowns for delivery. Presumably, he'd give half up front, and then the receiving party would pay half upon receipt. Allistair is allowing us to keep the 250, and then paying an additional 500."

"We're getting 750 crowns for this? What are we moving?" A fee like that was generally reserved for some very high-end merchandise. Usually only slavers got that kind of scratch, and Sora would sooner kill a slaver than take money from one. Maybe kill them and then take the money. That would be okay.

"An artifact, as I told you. I assure you it's a straight courier job."

She narrowed her eyes. "What kind of artifact?"

"I can't give you details yet, I'm afraid." He looked at her suspicious gaze and seemed to decide something. "Allistair seeks a book. That's all I can tell you."

Sora grunted. "I knew it was a magical thing! A spellbook? Necromancer's grimoire? What?"

Xezia laughed. "Not a spellbook exactly. No necromancy, I promise. But there's no more I can tell you."

"You wizards are so shifty. The lot of you."

"I'm not a wizard. I'm a mage. You know that."

"Oh, what's the difference? You're all drunk on magical power."

"A mage has a higher calling. For some, it's their Sovereign; for me, it's my Goddess."

"You're telling me Epi wants you to smuggle and steal? Somehow that doesn't seem like it's quite the province of a purity goddess."

"I don't question Epi's signs. I just follow them."

"Yeah, okay," Sora replied, unconvinced, "if you say so."

Xezia

It is said that a man with many names has associates, not friends.

So it was with Xezia (as he was currently known), but he had as many faces as he had names, thanks to his skill in magical disguises, so even if he had had friends in years past, they would no longer recognize him.

Xezia saw friendships as distractions, so not having any was a boon, not a burden. That is not to say he didn't enjoy companionship, he just preferred associations of convenience rather than creating deeper ties.

He thought about this as Sora walked beside him. In truth, she was probably the closest thing to a friend he'd ever had, since they'd been traveling together for the better part of a year. She knew his personality quirks, his sense of humor, and what made him angry. She knew when to chat and when to leave him alone. She was genuine and without pretense, and against his better judgement, he actually trusted her ... not just because she owed him a blood debt, but because she had a sense of honor. Even though she would undoubtedly go her own way as soon as she found a way to settle up her debt to him, she would watch out for him and never betray him, even under duress.

Xezia found this both comforting and discomforting at the same time. Trust was a foreign commodity to him. He knew he could not be trusted, and assumed the same of everyone he met. Sora had wrinkled his world view. He almost felt bad for not giving her mission details. Almost.

"I wouldn't trust just anyone with this mission, Xezia. I need to know that you are 100% committed to the cause." Being hand-chosen by Allistair was both an honor and a curse. It showed his confidence in you, but it also meant he felt that you could handle the most dangerous situations.

"You know you have my loyalty," Xezia replied carefully.

"I do indeed; otherwise, you'd have been dead long ago. Can you trust this elf you're traveling with?"

"I trust her with my life, but not your information."

Allistair grinned wickedly. That had been the answer he wanted, as Xezia well knew.

"This book is not to be trifled with. You must not, under any circumstances, let it fall into the hands of Ironshield. It would be better to destroy it than to let those genocidal maniacs have it."

"If I may ask, what is this book?"

Allistair leaned forward as if sharing a secret, though no one was in the room but the two of them. "We suspect it is the wizard Zaos Craxinna's research. He believes he's located the Book of Order."

Xezia's jaw dropped open. "I thought that was just a myth."

"Everyone thinks that, which is why the Books have remained safe for hundreds of years. But Godfroy has developed an unhealthy obsession for them, and he appears to have some help in finding them, our sources say."

"Wait," Xezia sputtered, holding up his hand. "Are you telling me ALL the Holy Books are real?" All Xexia could think of was his Goddess, and what this might mean for his connection with her.

"We believe so. And since you have proven yourself clever, loyal, and ruthless, the Black Moon is entrusting you with the honor of retrieving this research, if that's what the package is, and then finding and bringing the Book of Order directly to me."

Betraying the Black Moon, and Allistair in particular, was foolhardy. The crime lord had ways of knowing things: spies abounded, and Xezia suspected that he had some telepathic abilities as well. At any rate, there was no way Xezia could steal the book for himself. But surely there was some way to gain something other than the generous fee Allistair was offering. How could he possibly have even temporary possession of such a powerful item without finding some way to exploit its magic?

Xezia ran his tongue along the inside of his cheek as he always did when he was thinking deeply about something.

"What are you up to?" Sora asked, startling him out of his thoughts. She narrowed her amber eyes at him. "You're plotting."

A smirk threatened to make an appearance, but he held it back. "No, no. I'm just wondering how many others will show up to try and complete this job. I've no concern about potential criminals, mind you, but the last thing we need is some over-confident hero whose dead-set on 'doing the right thing'."

"Isn't that what the assassin is for?"

"Indeed. But it's good to consider as many potential permutations of the situation as we can in advance."

Sora stopped walking and turned toward Xezia with her hands on her hips. "I think you're trying to figure out how to steal this artifact spell book thing."

Damn her for knowing him so well, even though she knew nothing of his past. "Don't trouble yourself with that. My brain does what it does. I'm not stupid enough to betray Allistair."

"Good, because if I have to die paying my blood debt because you're being an imbecile, I'll come back as a wraith and haunt you till you go mad." She stomped ahead of him, but he knew she really wasn't angry. She was watching out for him, in her own way. Xezia shook off the thought and the pleasant feeling that arose from having someone even seem to care what happened to him.

Damn her.

Ren

Ren strolled along beside Dalgis, greatly enjoying the beast's company. He had a decidedly pleasant demeanor and positive outlook, both rare qualities in the world these days. The constant threat of Ironshield to the other kingdoms, especially to Rosend and Heavenly Skies, had a tendency to sour people's moods, particularly the closer one got to the border they shared with Godfroy's kingdom. Being visibly human himself, Ren rarely encountered problems even when he came in contact with traveling bands of soldiers, but his new companion would likely raise quite a few eyebrows, and even more questions.

"So tell me, Dalgis my friend, how did you come to be all alone in this part of the world? Wouldn't you be much safer farther from Ironshield's borders?"

"A very fine question, friend. I had, indeed, for several years in my youth, retreated to the most wooded region in the southwestern corner of Heavenly Skies, since so many different species dwell there, but recently, I've come into the notion that it's rather cowardly of me to hide away after Ironshield murdered my family."

"Do you seek to take on Godfroy's army all by yourself? That seems rather ill-advised, if you don't mind my saying so, though it would be quite a sight to see." Ren smiled at the thought of Dalgis sweeping through a unit of shocked Ironshield soldiers.

"Ah, yes, your concern is justified, Sir Knight. I admit that I have no mind for strategy. But I could remove a few of Ironshield's patrols here and there. It may not bring Godfroy to his knees, but it might present some inconvenience."

"I admire your spirit, Dalgis. Perhaps it was destined somehow that we were to meet. Once I complete my friend's errand, perhaps you and I can find a way to disrupt as many of Godfroy's plans as our time in this life allows."

Dalgis laughed, an odd sound somewhere between a bellow and a honk. "I like the sound of that, indeed! I shall assist you in your task, and then together, we shall rain great suffering on King Godfroy's wicked armies!" He was getting quite excited. "Wait just a moment ... I just realized that you're human. Are you not of Ironshield yourself, Sir Ren?"

"Ah, I was wondering when that might come up. I am of blended parentage, but my features are human. That helps avoid a great deal of direct confrontation, and that's an advantage. I assure you that I have no love for Godfroy or his goals. Ironshield, though still a predominantly human kingdom, had no widespread hatred for other races until that impostor took the throne."

"Impostor, you say?"

"Yes, Godfroy was not in the line of succession of the royal Talon family. He and his band of zealots slaughtered their way down the Talon family tree. If any folks of royal blood survived, which is unlikely, they fled for their lives and scattered." There was bitterness in Ren's voice.

"You sound as if you remember it personally, friend."

"I do indeed, Dalgis. I was a young man at the time, barely fourteen. My mother was a nursemaid to the Talon family, and when Godfroy's crazed troops stormed the palace, we were lucky to escape with our lives. We managed to remain together, but we never saw anyone we knew from the palace again. I have heard, in the years since, that several of the other staff members survived, and there are rumors that some of the more distant Talons went into hiding."

"Have you sought any of them out?" Dalgis asked, entranced by Ren's sad tale.

"No, no. If I were to find them, that might put them in danger. Best for them to remain lost to time so they may live out their days. I do grieve, though, for the good friends that I lost, and I pray that they are safe somewhere in the world."

"That is a heartbreaking story, Sir Ren." Dalgis sniffed loudly, and Ren could see the tears in his eyes. "We shall make them pay for what they've done to both of us."

Ren smiled and patted Dalgis's back. "We have only known each other for a little over a day, and I count you as a true friend, Dalgis. Godfroy's men won't know what hit them. The sun is only a short time from setting, and I'd say we are less than two hours' walk from Zaos's tower. I hate to stop when we are so close, but these woods are not good to traverse in the darkness. If Zaos has not already left, he won't be leaving today. Shall we camp for the night and set out at dawn?"

"A marvelous suggestion, Sir Ren. I shall go see if I can't just hunt something up for our evening meal. Perhaps you can start a fire?"

"That I will."

Dalgis trotted off deeper into the forest in search of a meal, and Ren couldn't help thinking that this unusual creature was by far the finest companion he'd ever had. The fact that he shared Ren's desire to wreak chaos down on Ironshield was a bonus. In time, Dalgis returned with a deer clamped in his powerful jaws. Ren gladly butchered the animal and cut most of the meat into chunks for his new friend. He cooked his own portion on the fire and they ate heartily.

As the fire died down to a glow, Dalgis flopped down and fell asleep, breathing rhythmically through his snout. The sound resembled the crashing of waves. Ren leaned against Dalgis's rib cage and was lulled to sleep by dreams of the sea.

The knight and the beast made good time toward the tower, and arrived while the morning sun was only a little above the horizon. Dew still glistened on the ivy and moss that clung to the stone walls.

"This is a rather disappointing tower," Dalgis commented. "I expected something much more grand."

He wasn't wrong. Zao's tower looked more like a three-story box. The gray stone walls were not exactly crumbling, but they weren't properly squared off, giving the building a rather droopy appearance. The grounds, if they could be called that, were littered with wagon parts and random bits of wood and metal, but the grass was perfectly manicured and almost unnaturally green.

At the edge of the clearing, a female sun elf and what looked to be a male human in a sizable cloak sat on discarded barrels, chatting quietly to each other. When Ren and Dalgis entered the clearing, the pair looked up with wide eyes.

"Well, hello there!" called Dalgis, in his usual cheery voice.

Ren was immediately suspicious of the pair, but plastered a smile on his face to match his friend's demeanor. He had expected that Zaos might try to transport the research himself, but it appeared that others might have received the same summons Ren had. The elf wore a short-sleeved tunic and a leather breastplate, leather breeches and high boots. Her muscular arms revealed her warrior nature, as did the fact that her fighting hand rested loosely on the pommel of the longsword at her side as she surveyed Dalgis through narrowed eyes.

The man at her side drew back his hood, revealing ears that came to a small point. Not fully human, then, but not fully elf… or were those orcish ears? It was difficult to tell. But the man stepped forward, raising a hand in greeting. "Good morning! What brings you here?"

"I've come to run an errand for my friend," Ren replied, careful not to give any details to this stranger.

"I see! We've come for the same reason. Zaos must have asked far and wide for assistance. Or perhaps he just felt that a larger party was necessary to complete his task. My name is Xezia, and this is my associate Sora."

"Well met!" said Dalgis. "Please forgive me for not shaking hands. Somehow, it seems rude to shake with a claw." Dalgis grinned, which came off comical rather than threatening somehow, despite his sharp and cone-shaped teeth. He leaned back on his haunches and raised his arms, wiggling his foreclaws to demonstrate. The elf laughed.

"What in the wide world are you?" she asked, but there was mirth in her eyes.

"My species has no name, my lady, as I am the only one of my kind. I am simply Dalgis." He bowed deeply.

"Well met to you, too, Dalgis."

Ren cleared his throat. "And I am Ren, wayward and wandering would-be knight, at your service." He bowed slightly, but kept his eyes up, prepared for any sudden or unexpected movements.

"Well, isn't this cozy?" came a voice from the trees. Ren spun around and squinted toward the sound, spotting what appeared to be a teenage girl nestled into the crook of a tree at the edge of the woods.

"Good gracious, child. What are you doing up there?"

"Same as you, sounds like," she replied, acrobatically swinging herself down from the branches and landing with barely a *fwp* on the hard ground. "A man is paying big crowns to have a package delivered, so I'm here to do the job. I really don't think all of you extra folks are going to be necessary."

Ren chuckled at her bravado. "Somehow, I doubt you'll be able to convince the four of us of that. Or, and I mean no offense, to entrust such a big job to such a wisp as yourself."

The girl tossed her blue-black hair and narrowed her eyes at him. "You'd do well not to underestimate me."

He stifled the laugh rising in his throat. She was a tiny thing, but she seemed so very confident. He was almost convinced that she might, indeed, be a threat. She walked past him and up to Sora. "Nice sword," she said matter-of-factly.

"Don't get any ideas, girl," Sora warned.

The girl smiled and winked at her.

"Speaking of underestimating," Xezia commented, "you'd do well to heed my friend's warning. She's really fond of that sword. What should we call you?"

"I'm not sure you should call me anything," the girl quipped.

"Now, now, that's not very friendly." Everyone started at the sound of a new voice from the doorway of the tower. Leaning on the doorframe was a shapely raven-haired woman in a split-skirt riding outfit and a traveling cloak.

Ren looked back and forth from the girl to the woman. "Where in the world did you come from? And are you two related?"

The woman laughed, a silvery sound that was almost musical. "I'm from everywhere, friend, and you clearly have a human's sense of smell, or you'd never have asked me that question."

"What in the world is that supposed to mean?" Ren asked, feeling as though he should, perhaps, be offended.

"She means," Dalgis offered, "that they are different species. The tiny one smells like a mammal, and the bigger one smells a bit like a reptile, though not exactly. Fascinating."

"Back to the first question," Xezia chimed in. "Where did you come from? And don't be cute; we don't mean your origin. We mean just now."

"Oh, now don't feel all threatened because a little lady like me managed to sneak by you when you were preoccupied with the tot there."

"I'm not a tot," the girl sneered.

"Don't take offense, my dear. You're clearly much younger than any of us. Let us begin again. My name is Daijera, and I have also come to assist the wizard in the delivery of his item. If I'm completely honest, I'm surprised there weren't a few more takers. The fee was quite generous."

"Fee?" Ren sputtered. "The old fool offered up a fee?" *Unbelievable.* Zaos had sent for him, and then advertised openly to anyone who might want some money. It was almost a guarantee that one (if not all) of these people were criminals.

"Who are you calling an *old fool*?" A resonant, yet clearly aged voice rang out from one of the windows above. The party's eyes turned upward to see a grizzled old man in ochre robes leaning out with a stern expression. "Right on time, right on time. Excellent."

Ekko

The strange-looking woman had been correct. There had been other interested parties. And at least three of them were sleeping soundly on the side of the road from Galantus, small darts with tsetse venom in their necks. It was to be expected that there would be a group already here, but it didn't seem fair to Ekko that these *people* stood in the way of her big payday.

She didn't play well with others. Others had a tendency to betray you and leave you rotting in jail. And then you ended up on the run for months. She gritted her teeth and brooded. *Always watch your own back*, she reminded herself.

That said, she did like the beast. He looked fun. She wondered if he'd let her ride him like a steed. It might be worth traveling with this party for a little while just for that.

The old man disappeared from the window and, after what seemed to Ekko an interminable amount of time, he opened the door where Daijera had been standing.

"Come in, come in, friends. Have a seat and I'll fetch some wine, and we shall discuss business." Ekko passed through the doorway and scanned the room, which was dimly lit by sunlight streaming through the small windows. The room was roughly rectangular with a door leading to a second room on the right wall and a rickety iron-and-metal staircase attached precariously to the opposite wall which clearly led to some sort of quarters above. No doubt that's where the old wizard had been when he greeted them out the window. Despite Zaos's suggestion to sit while he brought refreshment, there was, alas, nowhere to actually take a seat. Every horizontal surface was covered in papers, books, and random bits of spell-casting ingredients.

The man in the armor (Ren, was it?) spoke up. "Zaos, you owe me a bit of an explanation. You wrote to me for help, but then it appears you put out a flyer to anyone and everyone who might like to take your money, and potentially leave you dead and thoroughly robbed in the process. Have you gone completely round the twist?" He paused. "No offense intended to any of you, of course."

"None taken," Daijera responded, amusement twinkling in her unusual green eyes. Ekko noticed that the woman was leaning against a table with an assortment of crystals spread across it. She also noticed that there was a small outlined shape free of dust amidst the collection. Hm. It seemed to Ekko that she might have a little competition. As she thought this, Daijera's eyes met hers ... and winked.

Dalgis

There were times when being enormous was an advantage, and then there were times when it was a decided disadvantage. This was one of the latter times.

Dalgis had plopped himself outside the open door as soon as it became apparent that his body would not fit through the narrow door frame. He extended his neck and head into the room so that he might feel like part of the conversation, but it wasn't the most comfortable arrangement.

Zaos was pouring wine for each of the people in the room, but when he came around to Dalgis, he paused.

"Oh, dear. Do you drink wine? Would you prefer water?"

"That is most considerate of you. A bowl of water would be most appreciated." He suddenly looked around self-consciously. "Glasses are, regrettably, rather difficult for me to hold, and my claws get stuck if I try to use mugs or tankards."

"No explanation is necessary, Dalgis," the wizard smiled and patted Dalgis on the neck. He shuffled off and returned with a bowl about half full of water.

Dalgis accepted it gratefully with outstretched arms. He bent his neck at a surprising angle and managed to pour the water into his mouth. It wasn't a perfect job; maybe a third of the water splashed to the floor. But he had drunk his water the *civilized* way, and he was terribly proud of himself.

All conversation had been suspended while everyone watched the spectacle, but once he was done, Zaos picked right back up where he'd left off.

"As I said, Ren, I didn't doubt your dedication, but I couldn't be certain you would be able to make it here in time, and the package really needs to leave here today to ensure that it can reach Kieran before he leaves for his month-long stay in Galantus."

"Is this Kieran fellow the intended recipient of your package?" Xezia asked. "How many days' journey will it be to reach him?"

"Yes, yes indeed. He has a cottage perhaps two long days' journey from here, outside of Wheatfields. The route is a relatively dangerous one, so it's probably a good thing that you have numbers on your side." Zaos opened a large wardrobe near the back of the room and pulled out a chest approximately the size of a saddlebag. "This is the package which needs to be delivered into Kieran's hands. It must not be given to anyone else. If you cannot give it to him, please bring it back here to me."

"I don't mean to be crass," Xezia began, "but I believe there was a mention of payment?"

"Indeed, indeed," said the wizard, distractedly. "Of course, I must protect my interests as well ... I will give you each 50 crowns as a down payment for services rendered, and Kieran will pay you each another 50 when you deliver the package safely into his hands."

"That's a lot of money; even more than you originally offered," the young girl said. "How do you know we won't run off with it and leave your package in the woods somewhere?"

"There is no certainty of that, of course," Zaos replied, "but I would like to believe in the better nature of people. I have taken appropriate magical measures to protect it from being lost or being opened by anyone other than Kieran."

"I am quite certain we can get this package to your friend, good sir," Dalgis said. "This is a stalwart company indeed."

The girl gritted her teeth and pressed her lips together. Then she turned to Zaos. "Do we get to know what's in it?"

"No, my dear, I don't think I will share that with you. What I will tell you is that it is of little to no value to anyone outside of a very small circle of individuals."

"Wizards," Sora muttered.

Zaos half nodded. "Indeed, but only a select group of them. The package truly has no monetary value at all."

"Well, I would say," Dalgis began, "that the contents of the chest are irrelevant. All we need to know is where to take it and who should receive it."

"Dalgis, I can see that you are a ... an individual of honor. I can see why my old friend Ren would find you pleasant company." He handed the box to Ren, who had remained uncharacteristically silent throughout the exchange. "I shall entrust this to you, my friend, and I hope that you shall come back and visit with me once your task is done. I have much to tell you about Ironshield's recent movements."

Ren accepted the box and nodded curtly, and it seemed to Dalgis that perhaps he was offended by the wizard tasking these strangers to accompany him on this mission. No matter; Dalgis felt certain that Ren's good humor would return once they were back on the road. What could be better than traveling with an interesting band of individuals? It had been a good while since he had had any friends, and he relished learning about each and every one of them.

Chapter Three

The Wagon

Xezia

Drat. Not only had the elderly wizard bespelled the package in who-knows-how-many ways, he had also handed it to the knight to carry. This was just becoming unnecessarily difficult. Not insurmountable, of course, and Xezia had known that it was likely that other parties would show up to try and get involved with the package, but the moment that the knight showed up with that ... what the devil was it? ... Xezia knew the normal method of charm and manipulation wouldn't be enough.

He probably should have anticipated that the book, if that's indeed what it was, would be under some sort of protection magic.

He turned new ideas over in his mind. If he could somehow get possession of the book for an extended period, he could probably find a way to weasel his way through the spells the wizard had cast. If he couldn't get his hands on the book because of the sheer number of people present, could he and Sora steal it back from this Kieran fellow? There was always abject slaughter of the other party members, but he wasn't sure whether the girl (who still hadn't revealed her name) or Daijera was the assassin the Black Moon had sent. Daijera seemed the more likely candidate, but she didn't exactly carry herself like a contract killer. And while the kid seemed a bit young for the role, one could never be sure. Plus, she seemed a lot more shifty. The mage sighed. There was just no alternative. He and Sora would just have to travel with these strangers for a little while until he was able to gather a bit more information.

They'd been walking for several hours without incident. No one seemed to want to socialize or get to know each other, except for Dalgis. He seemed to crave conversation, and it really didn't matter what the topic was. He had chatted with Sora about her time sailing the Dividing Sea; he had asked Daijera about her parentage, and she had deftly switched the subject and instead told him a story about how Hohn, the Goddess of Life, had celebrated the creation of the bipedal races by hosting a parade of multicolored elephants and making them all walk on their back legs to the amusement of the newly-formed humans, elves, goblins, dwarves, and orcs.

The girl scouted ahead and generally avoided conversation, sometimes disappearing into the woods for a half hour at a time, but now she walked beside Dalgis, having to almost jog so that her petite legs could keep pace with his huge ones. It sounded like she was trying to convince him to let her ride on his back.

"So, which one do you think it is?" Sora whispered to Xezia in the strange sun elf dialect that sounded like unintelligible mumbling to anyone who didn't speak the language.

"I think the woman is more likely, but I'm keeping my eye on both her and the child," he whispered back

Sora nodded. "I don't think I like either of them."

Xezia smirked. "Of course you don't, and the truth is that you don't have to. The bigger problem is trying to figure out if that package contains the cargo Allistair wants or not."

At the sound of Allistair's name (which didn't translate completely into Sun Elvish), even in whispers, Daijera looked over her shoulder and winked. Then she turned her back again.

"I guess that settles that," Sora mumbled. "She must have really good hearing."

"She must. But at least it appears she's with us. How long would it take you to do a thought push?" It wasn't a well-known fact, but sun elves had the unique ability on sunny days to, after a few minutes of concentration, send a few words or mental images to a designated target. It was a useful technique when hunting on their native ground in the northern plains of Benedictus, but it was indispensable in any kind of clandestine activity.

"Probably about five minutes. It's pretty sunny today. What do you want me to send?"

"I haven't quite decided. I'll let you know when I figure it out."

The two of them walked in silence for a few more minutes, the drone of Dalgis and the girl's chatter providing an ebb and flow of quiet sound.

"Attention, everyone," the beast announced from the front of the party, "I'd like to introduce my new friend, Ekko!"

The girl looked sourly over her shoulder at the rest of the group and then back at Dalgis. "Okay, so now you have to keep your end of the bargain," she said.

Dalgis's honking chuckle carried throughout the woods, and he stopped walking long enough to lower his shoulder so that Ekko could scramble up and ride on his back.

They camped for the night and, although the party set up a watch, Xezia and Sora made sure that one of them was awake during each shift. It just so happened that Xezia and Ren happened to be on watch at the same time.

"Well," the mage began conversationally, "this is a strange method of organizing a paid task, wouldn't you agree?" He sat on a log a few feet from Ren near the fire.

"It is indeed," Ren replied in a surly tone without offering up any additional information.

"Did I gather correctly that you knew Zaos from before this?"

"Yes; we've known each other for maybe 15 years. I don't know him well, but I met him when he was still traveling regularly to the Galantian Library. There are a number of wizards who do research there, and he was one of the more prominent ones until perhaps two years ago."

"So you've found him to be an upstanding fellow, then? You believe him to be honest about the contents of this package?"

"I do indeed. Zaos has no reason to lie about anything. He serves Utrui."

Xezia's heartbeat quickened. If Zaos served the God of Order, then the intelligence Allistair had received about the package might well be credible. "I had not realized he was a mage. May I see the chest? Under your direct supervision, of course," he added. He mustn't overplay his hand.

Ren studied him for a long moment. "What did you say your business was on this errand again?"

Xezia smiled, and did his best to make it look friendly. "In truth, friend, I am trying to earn a bit of money. Sora and I have been traveling together for some time, as you may have guessed. We ran into some bandits perhaps a month ago, and while we were not severely injured in the attack, they did get away with most of our crowns, and several gems I had in my possession. I am a servant of Epi, you see, and I was traveling between temples with Sora as my protector." The half-truth slid across his tongue as easily as fine wine.

At the mention of Epi, Ren raised his eyebrows. "I wouldn't have pegged you for an Epi mage."

"I am indeed," Xezia pulled out his obsidian holy symbol, which glinted black against the darkness. "I swore my life to Epi when zealots of Ipthel destroyed my village."

That part was true. He was left as nearly the only survivor of the raid. As he had watched the flames engulf his once-peaceful village thirteen years ago, while the wails of the dying rang in his ears, he had sworn to serve the goddess of purity and do whatever it took to destroy the followers of Ipthel wherever he crossed their path.

Ren's expression softened slightly. "I have run into Ipthel followers before. They are a brutal band." His far-off expression told Xezia that Ren had indeed witnessed the brutality and wanton destruction the devotees of the God of Corruption left in their wake. "I can see why you would pledge yourself to Epi after that." He eyed Xezia once more, then reached into his pouch and passed the box over to Xezia so he could look at it.

It was heavier than Xezia had expected. He held it in his hands and inspected the smooth, dark wood, bound in bands of what appeared to be iron. It was perhaps the size of two boot prints, roughly square, and as he turned it over in his hands, he could feel the soft *thwp* of an object inside. His tongue traced shapes against the inside of his cheek as he ran his thumb along the iron bands. "There doesn't appear to be a lock, a clasp, or even hinges," he commented, more to himself than to the knight sitting opposite him.

Ren shrugged. "I noticed that," he said simply. "The lid doesn't come off, though. It appears that Zaos did cast some sort of sealing spell on it. Magic isn't my specialty, but I can tell you that this chest is most assuredly not going to open to brute force."

Xezia wondered how Ren could know that, but was careful not to appear too interested. He forced a chuckle. "Tried to get it open, did you?"

Ren smiled a little. "During one of our little rest stops today, I did. Can you blame me for being curious?"

"Not at all," Xezia replied, and this time his smile was genuine. There was more to this knight than he had thought at first blush.

Daijera

The secret to a successful quest is having the right shoes. It was that simple. One must know what sort of mission one is on, and then dress accordingly. The mistake so many mediocre Black Moon associates made when taking on a mission like this one was trying too hard, particularly with disguises and creating alternate identities. The truth of the matter, Daijera had learned, was that if one kept a low enough profile and moved around a good bit, there was rarely a need for any type of disguise, save for the minor glamour of tinting her skin and camouflaging her slitted eyes.

And then there was the costuming part of disguises. So many new agents went overboard, trying to show off how skilled they were at dressing like a sailor, or a soldier, or a beggar. They'd spend a fortune on having just the right outfit, and often that outfit would stand out because it was too new, or didn't smell right, or was regionally incorrect. All that really mattered was choosing the right footwear for the task at hand.

In this case, she had had just enough time to buy an excellent pair of walking boots. Soft, durable, with strong, supportive soles and no height to the heels. It was foolish to try and look like something she wasn't, and the extra effort usually ruined the mission. So she simply played an exaggerated version of herself: a skilled musician and entertainer with charm to spare. The only thing she'd add, if anyone bothered to ask, is that she was traveling from town to town, performing and seeing the world, and she'd taken this job as a courier because the fee would assure that she could stay in nice inns instead of the dives she'd end up staying in with the money she currently had. It was convincing because, in large measure, it was true.

It had been fairly easy to spot the Black Moon operatives when they approached the tower; there was no chance that a beast like Dalgis was working for Black Moon. If his unique appearance wasn't enough of a reason, his genuine and decent personality was a guarantee that he wouldn't approve of the organization or their methods.

She rather liked Dalgis, though. He was a bit like a very charming talking horse. She found herself wanting to adorn him like one might a palace pet. He certainly would look nice with a sparkly collar. It would set his plumage off so nicely. She'd have to find him something when they reached a city, if they were all together that long.

Xezia and Sora were exactly what Daijera had come to expect of Black Moon smugglers. They were a formidable pair, actually. The best smugglers never looked like smugglers. Xezia was clearly a mage, which meant that either he was highly adept at healing or mind control, depending on which deity he served. Sora, though, was clearly a highly skilled melee fighter. Her leather armor held numerous weapons: some visible, like the sword and daggers she wore on her belt, and some hidden, like the finger blades and darts that were almost perfectly concealed along the edges of the shoulder guards and bracers she wore. Indeed, if Daijera hadn't been familiar with this sort of armor, she probably wouldn't even have known the tiny pockets were there.

When she had heard them muttering in some foreign tongue, she had made a point of listening in. Lamias had shockingly good hearing, due to their ability to sense sound vibrations as well as the typical noises that most people hear. She couldn't understand any of what they were saying, but when she heard something that sounded like "Allistair", she knew she'd pegged them correctly. She had shot Xezia a quick smile so he'd know she was the secret third member of the party. And hey, if she were mistaken about his identity, then he'd just think she was a flirt. That was okay, too.

The group of them had been following a trade road along the edge of some forest, and the traffic had been surprisingly sparse. They'd only passed a handful of travelers, most of whom were merchants traveling across Rosend in the direction of the Dividing Sea, presumably to some port to pick up or deliver merchandise. So it wasn't worrisome at first when she spotted the wagon near the side of the road a few hundred feet ahead, with a stocky male human working on one of the wheels.

Ekko was the first to notice that something seemed amiss.

"That wheel isn't broken," she hissed to the group, and then disappeared into the woods.

Dalgis and Ren, who were leading the way, slowed their pace, and deliberately didn't look in the direction Ekko had gone. Xezia, Sora, and Daijera tightened up the space between the party members as they walked at a slow, but normal pace.

"She's right," Ren said. "Do you think she's doing reconnaissance or flanking them?"

"I'd bet money on the latter," Sora smirked.

"I'll go back her up," Daijera decided and slipped into the treeline in the direction Ekko had followed. As she moved among the trees, she tied her split skirt behind her so that it somewhat resembled a tail. She had no intention of getting into hand-to-hand combat, but one could never be too careful. She moved stealthily through the underbrush and the not-so-broken wagon came into view to her left.

Above her, she heard a soft and unusual bird call, one that shouldn't have been native to these woods. She froze in place and searched for the source of the sound. She spotted Ekko above her and about half the distance to the wagon. Ekko had clearly been scrambling through the tree branches rather than on the ground; she held up two fingers and then made a hand gesture to bushes on either side of the wagon. Sure enough, it appeared that two figures were hunched down and lying in wait for unwary travelers. Ekko pointed to the more distant of the two, then to herself. Daijera nodded and pointed to the closer one. Once she had received acknowledgement of the plan, Ekko resumed her advance through the trees, making no more noise than a squirrel.

Daijera had to move a little more slowly because of the thick ground cover. Keeping an eye on her target, she drew her blowgun and three darts quietly out of her pouch as she approached. Once she was about 15 feet away, she hunkered in place and held the bunch of darts in front of her lips. She opened her mouth wide, loosening the membrane on the venom sac. When she felt the venom start to flow, she blew heavily on the dart tips, coating them with poison. She loaded one dart into the blowgun and looked over to where Ekko waited in the tree directly above the second henchman, her daggers drawn and at the ready.

It was only a few seconds before Dalgis's voice rang out in greeting to the man pretending to fix the wagon. "Ho, there, friend! Can we lend some assistance?"

"Yes indeedy!" came the man's raspy reply. Daijera leaned a little lower so she could look beneath the brush that was providing her cover, and she saw the man nod ever-so-slightly to the two concealed figures. Then he knocked four times on the wagon wheel spoke, and Daijera saw the curtain at the back of the covered wagon rustle.

More of them, she thought. *I wonder how many?* The four knocks, she was sure, indicated the number of members of the approaching party to the hidden assailants in the wagon. *Excellent. They don't know about the two of us.* She looked up at Ekko and the girl nodded. She had noticed the code as well. Despite the oncoming conflict, Daijera smiled in admiration. This near-child was incredibly capable for one so young.

As the party drew closer, the man stood to greet them, and the hidden attackers slowly drew back their bows. The time for action had come; Daijera and Ekko had to hope that the party was well-prepared for combat. Daijera raised the blowgun to her lips and raised her fingers in countdown: *3-2-1.*

When she finished the countdown, she fired her dart, striking the archer in the neck behind his ear. His arrow flew wide, well off target, warning the party of the possibility of more concealed attackers. She heard a cry of pain as, no doubt, Ekko dropped with her daggers on the other archer. Daijera loaded the second dart and fired it just as her target turned around in alarm. The second dart lodged in his cheek. She cursed her aim, as she'd been aiming for his eye, but the toxin had already begun to do its work. The man began to gasp for air as the muscles in his throat became paralyzed. He dropped to the ground, and she knew he would never rise again.

Shouting and the sounds of clashing metal arose from the road, the party now having engaged with the man at the wagon and whoever had been concealed inside. Daijera loaded her third dart and headed toward the edge of the trees.

Sora was heavily engaged with one of the humans who had presumably leapt out of the wagon, and Xezia was muttering and making elaborate hand gestures toward an archer who had taken cover behind the horses. Ren was on the ground, grappling with what appeared to be a female elf who had a very nasty-looking blade aimed at his eye. There was a great deal of screaming coming from the wagon, into which Dalgis had reached his upper half. Sizing up her best shot, Daijera shot her final dart at the elf, who fought Ren for another few seconds, but then began to convulse and seize. He pushed her off of him, and within seconds, she was dead.

Ren

Ren rose and looked around for additional attackers, but saw none who weren't already engaged. He wasn't sure what had happened to the elf woman, but clearly one of his compatriots had assisted him ... not that he had needed the help.

He raised his sword and advanced on the wagon, which was rocking and shaking with the violence of what was occurring within. He knew he had to be careful not to injure Dalgis, but he also felt his first priority was to help his new friend.

Using the wheel spoke as a step, he climbed up and used his sword to cut away the rough fabric covering the wagon. As it fell away, he was initially taken aback by the bloodbath within. Dalgis had a human sword arm (still with sword in hand) in his powerful jaws, and had clearly eviscerated the assailant with his foreclaw. Once the cover fell off of the wagon, he snapped his neck sharply to the left and sent the arm flying into the road. One final member of the gang was cowering in the corner of the wagon screaming hysterically and dripping with his associate's gore.

"Ho there, Dalgis!" Ren called out. "Let us wait on dispatching this one to see if he has any vital information!"

At the sound of Ren's voice, Dalgis let out a honking bellow, but ceased his attack. "I shall watch this one to ensure it doesn't escape," the great beast snarled.

"Good man," Ren affirmed, and turned to see if Xezia or Sora needed any assistance. It appeared, however, that the skirmish was over. Sora was wiping her sword on the tunic of her fallen opponent, and Xezia was standing beside her, breathing heavily. A red stain was spreading across his left shoulder.

"Xezia, are you badly injured?" Ren called, hopping down off the side of the wagon.

Xezia shook his head. "Nothing serious. An archer in the trees caught me by surprise. I'll heal. She won't, though." The satisfied smirk on his face was to be expected when one was triumphant over another in battle, but there was a slight gleam in his eye that Ren had come to recognize in those who drew excitement and energy from a kill. Still, the kill was justified, so there was no reason for concern ... yet.

Daijera and Ekko came out of the woods from separate positions and surveyed the carnage on the road.

"Dalgis," Ren began, "bring our new friend over here, please."

Dalgis leaned forward to grab the young man's belt in his teeth, but the would-be attacker screamed and scrambled out of the wagon, throwing himself at Ren's feet. Sora and Xezia approached as the man begged for mercy.

Sora swore in her guttural language and spit on the ground next to the prostrate man. She looked up to find the rest of the party staring at her, except for Xezia, who was nodding. "Filthy dirt elf," she translated, as if that explained everything. She wrinkled her nose in distaste and went to examine the other bodies.

"I don't believe I've ever heard of a dirt elf," Dalgis stated, clearly confused by Sora's display of disgust.

"Dirt elf is a derogatory term for sand elves," Ekko explained and balanced herself on the edge of the wagon, poking at its gory contents with a stick. She reached in and pulled a hefty dagger off the mutilated body.

"Well, that doesn't seem very nice," Dalgis said. "I will grant you that they were trying to rob and possibly kill us, but I don't see a need to be insulting. Isn't Sora an elf?"

"There are four types of elves, Dalgis," Xezia replied. "Sora is a sun elf, but there are also sea elves, sand elves, and storm elves."

"What, pray, is the difference?"

"The primary difference is geographical. Sun elves are numerous and live all over Benedictus and Heavenly Skies, and some have even made their way into Rosend. If you've met an elf, it's most likely a sun elf. Sea elves live in and around the Dividing Sea, as the name would suggest. Some even live in flotillas of sailboats and rarely venture on land. I've never met a storm elf, but I know someone who has. They only live in the Salaam Mountains on the northern coast of Rosend, and they generally don't interact with anyone outside their domain. Then there are sand elves. Originally, they inhabited the desert and plains regions on Ironshield's southern border, and they intermarried and interbred with their human neighbors so extensively that they are at least as much human as they are elves."

"Does King Godfroy tolerate them, then? I was under the distinct impression that he hated any race that wasn't human."

"Tolerate isn't exactly the right word," Xezia explained. "Some sand elves choose to serve Ironshield because of their extensive relations. Others are pushed into servitude if they want to remain in their ancestral lands. Either way, the other elves dislike them because of Godfroy's maniacal desire to wipe out the elven races. That's why Sora has an issue with this lad here. She's had to fight sand elves in the course of ... doing business, and it sickened her."

"Both of the archers Ekko and I took out were sand elves," Daijera confirmed. "Mine had no papers or identification on him, but he had that curled ear that sand elves often have. Same ears on the other one. I don't know if Ekko checked him for papers."

"I checked him for everything," she called from the front of the wagon. She was ripping apart the bench seat. "There's a hollow area under this bench for loot, but they didn't have much. A few crowns, some arrows, and a map. Apparently they weren't even *good* thieves," she concluded derisively.

Dalgis appeared to be thinking very hard as he examined their captive, and Ren patted him on the shoulder. "How can we ascertain whether or not this one works for Ironshield?" Dalgis asked. "Does Ironshield hire miscreants?"

"They don't call him the Blood King for nothing," Ren replied. "That's what we're going to ask him about, in fact."

The elf had been face down on the road, trembling and weeping throughout Dalgis's education on elves. "I don't know anything," he mumbled into the ground. "I just did what Grail told me. He said we'd make some good money on this road."

"And who is Grail?" Ren asked.

"He was in charge. He was the one fixing the wheel." He pointed toward the human Sora had fought. "He just told me what to do ... said we'd make money ..."

"And who was the brains behind the plan?" Xezia interjected. "Definitely not that guy over there. This was one of the sloppiest ambushes I've ever witnessed. Did someone tell him to set up an ambush here?" He moved in aggressively and grabbed the elf's shoulder, hauling him up onto his knees. "Who was your friend there taking orders from?"

"Orders? What orders? I don't know anything about orders!" The elf's voice rose to a hysterical pitch. He had already been upset at seeing his cohort disemboweled. He began to hyperventilate. "I don't — I don't —" His eyes rolled back in his head and he passed out, going limp in Xezia's hand and then slipping to the ground.

"Well, that wasn't very helpful," Sora remarked as she unhooked the horse from its harness.

"Even if Ironshield is trying to stir up trouble," Ren offered, "I'd lay money that this fellow didn't know anything about it. He didn't seem the type to be trusted with important information. No stomach for it, you know."

"Should we kill him, do you think?" Ekko asked, walking up and handing the map to Ren.

"I don't think so," Daijera said. "I'm not squeamish about killing someone who needs it, but I don't particularly think this fool needs it. What he needs is a stiff drink. On the very remote chance that he does have some connection with Ironshield and their various disruptions into other kingdoms' stability, it might not be unwise to let him report his failure back to his superiors. He'd more likely run for the hills and never come back. Godfroy's generals don't look too kindly on failure. I do think we should take the horse, though. That, at least, might have some value."

Xezia was chewing on his lower lip, staring at the unconscious elf. Then he slowly nodded. "You're probably right."

"Shouldn't we bury the others?" Dalgis asked. "Even if they are criminals, it seems just wrong to leave them strewn about this way."

"I'm not sure it's wise to take the time to bury them, Dalgis," Ren replied, "though pulling them off the road is a good idea."

"I can get rid of the bodies," Xezia offered. "If you put them into a pile away from the trees, I can immolate them all to ash."

"Thought you were an Epi mage," Ekko sniped.

"Fire purifies," Xezia said simply and shrugged his shoulders.

It didn't take long. Sora, Ren, and Dalgis heaped up the bodies in the center of the road, and Xezia began to chant while the others watched, fascinated at the process.

The holy symbol around his neck almost seemed to pulse with life as the corpses burst into a blue flame and burnt to dust almost instantaneously. At some point in the process, the remaining elf must have come to and fled for his life, because when the bodies were gone, so was he.

Xezia

Fire purifies indeed.

As he chanted the incantation and gesticulated in the elaborate shapes necessary to mold the elements, he concentrated on delivering these bodies as a sacrifice. Surely Epi would smile on him and his compatriots for wiping such scum from existence. He had felt the acceptance of the sacrifice in the blue flame and the powerful hum of his holy symbol as the bodies disintegrated before his eyes. He could feel the divine blessing flowing through his veins like liquor.

It did bother him a bit that the other elf had escaped. Not because he was a highway bandit, no, that Xezia could understand. He even grudgingly agreed with Daijera's assessment that the man would have no useful information.

Rather, he was disgusted by the elf's ineptitude and weakness. It really was an affront that fools like that thought they were entitled to take what belonged to others. Then again, that kind of stupidity was why most criminals got caught.

And why Xezia didn't.

CHAPTER FOUR

WELCOME TO WHEATFIELDS

Sora

She was fully aware of how her reaction might appear to the group, and she probably ought to care, but once you'd seen your elven brothers and sisters die by the hands of sand elves under Ironshield's direction, it was pretty hard not to hate them. Besides, they had just tried to kill the party. It's not like this was a harmless family of sand elves traveling to market with a load of vegetables.

She grumbled to herself as she unharnessed the horse. She could tell by the its lean belly and the whip marks on its back (one of which appeared to be quite fresh) that the bandits had mistreated it, and that made her just hate the lot of them that much more. Mistreating a horse was about as high a sin as Sora could imagine. She removed the last of the strapping that attached it to the wagon and led it toward the edge of the woods so it could munch on some grass. While it chewed, she pulled elo paste out of her belt pouch and applied a small amount to the wound on the animal's back.

Once the horse seemed comfortable, she tied the reins to a tree branch and started walking back to the others. The body of the human archer who had shot Xezia lay on the ground with her neck bent at an unnatural angle. In fairness, she had it coming; if you try to ambush a group of travelers, you ought to be better prepared for them to fight back. Assuming that none of them would be wizards or mages is just careless.

Xezia had darkened an awful lot over the past year. It was sometimes hard to recognize him as the same man she'd met a year ago.

The breeze was just perfect. The sails billowed until they stood taut in the wind, and the ship began to cruise along, roughly hugging the coastline. The sea elves were expert sailors, of course, so Sora took the opportunity to position herself on the aft deck and soak up some sun as they cruised along with their shipment.

For once, she wasn't even smuggling anything illegal. Just a cargo hold full of rich fabrics ... and a well-concealed noblewoman who had asked to be smuggled out of Rosend to be reunited with her non-noble lover, who had been sent away and was now serving as a chambermaid in one of the finest houses in Benedictus. Not illegal, but the noblewoman's family was none too happy that she'd run off.

And then there was this mage. New guy ... seemed like a ladder-climber in Black Moon's organization. Allistair had personally sent him to see how Black Moon operations worked on the Dividing Sea. Sora wasn't too sure what to make of him. He seemed, well, ***ordinary.*** *His hair, eyes, and skin were all variations of the same shade of light brown, which stood in stark contrast to his vibrant blue and green mage robes. He was serious and intense, but when he did smile, it was rather infectious. It was also usually at the expense of someone else. At the moment, he was leaning on one of the railings near the pulpit, staring at the craggy coastline.*

"What did you say your name was?" she had asked him.

"I didn't," he replied curtly, but with a trace of a smirk.

"Don't be difficult. What should I call you? I know the business, and I don't care if it's your actual name or not, but I have to call you something."

He thought about this for a minute, and it seemed like another sarcastic remark was ready to fly, but then he thought the better of it. "You can call me Xezia, I think."

"Fine, then. I'm Sora. Allistair messaged me that I should introduce you to some of the boat captains friendly to Black Moon. Have you already met Captain Clew?"

"I have indeed. He seems quite capable."

"He is, but not if you're trying to move something large or dangerous. He won't move weapons," Sora instructed.

"I'm rather surprised Allistair gives him a choice in the matter."

"Yeah, well, if Clew were human, Allistair could probably put more pressure on him. But sea elves are fiercely independent, and it's less trouble to accommodate them if you want to do business. You heard about the ***Lady Marga,*** *I assume?"*

"The ship that sank with a full cargo or contraband elo fruit and all hands? That was what, three years ago?"

Sora nodded. "What you may NOT know about that story is that the Captain found that one of Allistair's minions had put false bottoms in the crates of elo, and were smuggling enchanted arrows. The captain had a NO WEAPONS rule, and knew that Allistair wouldn't let him live if he ditched the cargo, so he just sunk the whole boat and crew together."

"If the entire crew died, then how do you know that's what happened?"

"Because he burnt a very nasty message to Allistair into the decking while the boat was sinking. I was part of the salvage crew."

Xezia nodded and looked back at the shoreline as the boat skirted the coast. "So you're saying that sea elves — WATCH OUT!" Xezia launched himself in front of Sora and shoved her backwards as a spear dropped down at her from the cliffs above. The spear hit the deck with a thunk as the point drove itself several inches into the wood where she had been sitting. Now Xezia was pinned there with the spear piercing his robes.

Sora recovered from her surprise and leapt forward, whipping out a dagger and slicing the fabric of Xezia's robes to free him from the spear. Simultaneously, she cried out to the crew, raising the alarm.

Sora and Xezia dove behind a pile of fresh water barrels that had been lashed to the deck as the boat's crew jumped into action. Her heart thudding in her chest, she turned to the mage. "Wow, thank you. You saved my life."

For the first time, she saw Xezia smile ear-to-ear, beaming and genuine. "I guess I did. That pretty much means you owe me until you can save me back, right?"

Sora grinned back at him. "I guess so."

"This could take awhile," he winked.

Yeah, this was definitely taking a while. And it had been ages since she'd seen that grin.

Daijera

It was early evening when the party began to see the first houses on the outskirts of Wheatfield. Every half a mile or so, they'd spot a dirt track leading to a cottage, usually with its own vegetable garden and some random livestock. Daijera had never been in this part of Rosend before, but the word *quaint* definitely applied.

As they passed one such cottage, she spotted a young boy of maybe seven hanging upside down from a tree. He looked to be partly sun elvish, with his golden hair and tawny eyes, but his darker skin tone betrayed mixed parentage.

"Well, hello there," she greeted him.

He grinned, revealing a hole where one of his canine teeth should have been. "Hi," he responded cheerfully, and skillfully swung himself up onto the branch. He kicked his legs back and forth as he looked down at her. "You're strangers. I'm not really supposed to talk to strangers."

"That's pretty good advice, my young friend. Perhaps you could give us some directions. Can you tell me where Kieran lives? He's a wizard."

"Everybody around here knows Kieran. He comes into town and tells stories on festival day. And he can make medicines and do magic stuff."

"That does sound like who we're looking for. Can you direct us?"

"If you go back the way you came a little bit, you'll see a path leading off that way." The boy pointed west. "That path leads to Kieran's house. He didn't come to the market this week. He might not be home," he added. "What kind of animal is that?" he asked, pointing at Dalgis.

"Why, that's Dalgis. He's ... well ... he's just Dalgis. I'm not sure there's a proper name for what he is. Would you like to make one up?"

The boy's eyes lit up. "He has very pretty red and orange feathers on his face, but I also like the shiny, bumpy skin on his legs. Is he part bird and part lizard?"

"That and a few other things, I'd wager," Daijera smiled.

"Can we call him a Phoenix Lizard?"

"I think he'll like that very much. I thank you for your direction, Mr ..." Here she paused, hoping he'd offer up his name.

"Jasah," he replied quickly, then slapped his hands over his mouth. "I shouldn't tell strangers my name."

"Well, Jasah," she said, "my name is Daijera. If we meet again, we won't be strangers." She gave him her friendliest smile, and she could tell he was smiling back under his hands. She gave him a deep bow and turned to the group.

"My new friend tells me that Kieran's cottage is back that way. He also tells me that Kieran might not be home, as he missed market day this week." She paused meaningfully at this last bit of information, hoping they would take her hint that something might be amiss.

"Well, then, let us waste no time!" Dalgis burst out excitedly, and Jasah squeaked and nearly fell off his branch in surprise when he saw that his "phoenix lizard" could talk.

"I couldn't agree more," Daijera said. "Also, Dalgis, young Jasah here has decided to dub you a *phoenix lizard.*"

Dalgis let out a rumble of laughter that sounded like someone trying to shake an egg out of a goose. "Marvelous! I shall classify myself thusly if I ever need to name my species."

The boy scrambled down the tree and half-ran into the road, staring at Dalgis with his mouth agape. He was hopping from one foot to the other in excitement. "REALLY?"

"Yes, indeed, my good lad. No one has ever bothered to make up a name for my species since I am the only one. I think you have made an excellent categorization of my physical attributes."

All the big words left Jasah a bit confused, but no less enthusiastic. "Can I … can I touch your feathers?" he asked in a high-pitched whisper.

Dalgis grinned, and somehow all those teeth seemed friendly rather than predatory. "I shall do you one better, my boy," he said, lumbering over to where the child stood. He lowered his head almost to the ground, and Jasah reached out a hand, tentative at first, but once he felt the downy softness of Dalgis's feathers, he began to pet them gently, his mouth puckered into a tiny "o". "If you are very quick about it," Dalgis said sweetly, "you may pluck out one of my feathers and keep it."

"Oh, but won't it hurt you?" the boy gasped, astonished by Dalgis's offer.

"No more than plucking a hair from your own head would," he smiled. "Just pull one out quickly and it will hurt me hardly at all."

The boy looked back at Daijera, as if for confirmation, and she smiled and nodded. Jasah selected a feather that was nearly as long as his forearm, fiery red and orange. He looked back at Daijera. "Would you help me? I'm so afraid I'll hurt him by not pulling right."

Something inside Daijera ached at the tenderness of this child and the mirrored innocence in Dalgis's kindness to him. "Of course," she replied, and placed her hand over the boy's. With a quick and deft motion, she plucked out the feather and removed her hand, leaving the boy with his crimson treasure. He held it in his hand as though he held a key to a palace.

"Thank you, Mr. Dalgis," he whispered.

"You are most welcome, Jasah," Dalgis replied.

Daijera patted the child on the head and the party began walking toward the path Jasah had indicated. He barely looked up as they walked away because he couldn't take his eyes away from his prize.

Ren

Nearly as soon as they were out of sight of the main road, Kieran's cottage came into view. Unlike the other tidy farming cottages they'd seen, Kieran's looked as though it was built for functionality, not comfort. The walls were made of stacked logs like many of the other cottages, but instead of being reinforced with plaster and stone, the seams were haphazardly spattered with sealing plaster and mud. Moss and lichens grew thick in these cracks, giving the impression that the dwelling was in the process of being reclaimed by the forest.

Even in this ramshackle state, it was readily apparent that something was wrong. The door was not only wide open, it appeared to be hanging from only one hinge.

Ren held his arm out to stop the party's movement, but the others had already slowed because they had seen the door, too. Ren looked over his shoulder at the others. Ekko gestured toward the side of the house and quickly disappeared into the woods. A couple of minutes later, she returned.

"There's no one inside," she reported, "and it looks like there was a struggle. Furniture is overturned, and there are books everywhere. I also smelled blood." She stopped short as if she'd said something she hadn't meant to.

"What do you mean you smelled it?" Ren inquired.

"I ... have a very sensitive nose," she responded. Ren made a mental note to get more information about that slip-up later, and based on the faces of the party, everyone else had done the same.

"Well," Dalgis announced, "if no one is there, let us then survey the place and see if we can deduce what might have happened."

Ekko had, if anything, under-reported the disaster that awaited them inside. There didn't appear to be a single piece of furniture intact in the three-room dwelling. Books were more than just scattered; they were torn apart. Crockery lay shattered on the floor, and food was strewn across the remains of an up-ended table. A chest of about the size of a barrel lay on its side with the lid ripped off and several robes and cloaks dumped onto the ground.

Dalgis couldn't fit through the door, so he poked his head and neck inside while the others surveyed the damage. "Ekko was correct. There is blood here." He used his snout to point toward the doorway leading to another room.

Papers were spilling out the door Dalgis had indicated, and it appeared that this room had been some sort of study.

Broken glass from smashed bottles and vials littered the floor, so Ren drew his sword and began using the point to sift through the debris. Roughly three layers of paper deep, he uncovered several red, sticky stains.

"Looks like there was quite a fight in this room," he reported to the others. "Based on the amount of blood here, I'd say that either one person was injured gravely, or multiple people sustained smaller, but significant, wounds."

"All the blood smells human," Dalgis offered.

Ren returned to the main room to find Ekko and Daijera sifting through the debris while Xezia and Sora searched what appeared to be a bedroom.

"I found something," Ekko reported, and removed a small, well-concealed panel in the discarded lid of the chest. She drew forth a small leather-bound journal and flipped through its pages. Shrugging, she handed the book to Daijera.

"Looks like a cipher key," Daijera observed.

"A what now?" Dalgis asked.

"A cipher key. It's used to help translate an encoded document. Looks pretty complicated, too."

"Do you know much about codes and documents?" Ren asked, narrowing his eyes at her.

Daijera smiled, and for the first time, Ren noticed that her canines were slightly more pointed than those of most people. He began to question exactly how she came to be on this mission.

"I have a wide variety of skills. I'm an entertainer, and sometimes I find myself in the employ of noble households, individuals in leadership, and people in less-than-upstanding lines of business. I make it a point to gain useful skills and knowledge. I recognize this as a cipher key, but I have to confess that I don't rightly know what to do with it."

"You'd need a document to decode, I'd imagine," Xezia suggested, "and unless I miss my guess, that is what whoever ransacked this place was looking for. It was too well-hidden not to be important."

"I suspect you're right about that," Ren agreed, though he wasn't sure he bought Daijera's explanation. "Dalgis, can you tell how old the blood is?"

"I'm afraid that is beyond my skills, though I can tell you it isn't fresh."

Ekko ducked into the back room and returned within seconds. "From the look of it, it's been here several days, a week at the outside. The blood is thick and congealed, but not dry. Also, I can't be sure, because it's been tramped through a bit, but the pooling looks like a stab wound. If someone had been slashed, the blood would be sprayed around."

Ren nodded. Ekko's reasoning was quite sound, but he was beginning to wonder what kind of unsavory characters he had gotten himself in with.

"The sun is setting," he said. "I suggest we bunk here for the night and then make some inquiries in Wheatfields tomorrow morning. If we can't find Kieran or at least some lead on where he may be, we should return to Zaos with his package." The sooner he could return the package to the rightful owner, the better. The longer he traveled with this unusual band of people, the more he distrusted some of their motives, or their ethics at the very least.

"Marvelous plan, Sir Knight," Dalgis affirmed. "I shall make myself a fine bed out here in the woods and call for you at dawn." He withdrew his body from the doorway and disappeared into the trees.

Chapter Five

The Search for Kieran

Ekko

This was turning out to be a truly annoying job. It should have been very simple: pick up a package and some gold, deliver the package and get more gold. But not only was she now going to have to split the payout, the payday was delayed by at least three more days. The difference between having fifty crowns and having a hundred crowns was nothing to be ignored, though, so Ekko grudgingly decided to stick with the group for now.

Besides, Dalgis made a marvelous steed for someone her size. That made it worth staying for at least a few more days.

Speaking of Dalgis, he was true to his word and loudly greeted everyone in the small house just as the sun began to clear the horizon.

"Bright good morning, all! Shall we figure out a plan of action?"

"I had some thoughts about that," Xezia said. "Might it be wise for some of us to inquire about Kieran in town, while perhaps Daijera and Dalgis talk to some of the nearby residents to see if they saw or heard anything amiss in the last several days?"

Daijera nodded. "Good idea. We can start with Jasah and his family, since they seem to live the closest."

"I'll go with you," Ekko stated, "and I can check the surrounding woods for clues. I'm a pretty good tracker."

Everyone agreed, and after one more sweep of the cottage to make sure they hadn't missed anything, they positioned the broken door back in place and started back up the path toward the road. When they reached the tree where they had met Jasah the night before, Xezia, Sora, and Ren continued up the road toward Wheatfields while Daijera, Dalgis, and Ekko approached Jasah's modest home. Within the gate, chickens roamed freely around a small coop, clucking and pecking at the ground. Ekko's eyes lit up, and she had to remind herself that now was not the time to steal a nice, fat hen from the small yard.

"Perhaps I ought to stay back just a little," Dalgis offered. "I would hate to alarm the family."

Ekko patted Dalgis's knee and tried hard not to stare at the birds. "I'll wait here with you. Daijera can go talk to Jasah and his parents."

As Daijera approached the gate, the door swung open and a youthful woman stepped out. On her arm hung a basket of ground corn for the yard's tenants. She started at the sight of strangers at her gate.

Though visibly young, her skin and hair were the deep brown of tree bark, and Ekko realized at once where Jasah had gotten his unique coloring. It took Ekko a moment to realize that the woman was a dryad; it was so unusual to see one living in a house rather than within a tree deep in the woods.

"Good morning," Daijera greeted her. "We had the pleasure of meeting young Jasah last night on our way to find Kieran, and I was wondering if I might ask you a question or two."

"I suppose you can talk to me while I do my morning work," the woman replied, her eyes wary.

"I thank you," said Daijera in that charming way that she had. "We came into town to see Kieran, as I said, and when we arrived at the house, we found him not at home. It appeared that perhaps he might have left in a hurry, and may have been injured, and we're concerned about him. Could you tell me when you might have seen him last?"

"Kieran is a good neighbor," Jasah's mother said pointedly. "He keeps to himself. I believe it's been two market days since I've seen him. About eight days ago, I 'spect."

"Has anyone else come to see him of late?"

"Not so far as I know," she replied. "What did you say your business with him was?"

"I didn't say," Daijera smiled, "but we were bringing him a package. Do you know if he was planning to travel anywhere?"

She shook her head, seeming to soften a little in the bright glare of Daijera's smile. "Nope. Wish't I could tell you more. He sure is a good neighbor."

Just then, a gasp and squeak erupted from inside the house and Jasah came bounding out, pointing toward the yard gate. "You see, Mama? I told you there was a magnificent beast!" He puffed up his chest like an announcer at a carnival. "Behold the Phoenix Lizard Dalgis!"

Dalgis sputtered with a mixture of affection and amusement. "Well, good morning, young lad!"

Ekko took a few tentative steps toward the yard and peered over the gate. As if by instinct, the chickens squawked and scattered toward the coop.

"Hello, Jasah," Daijera greeted him. "I was just asking your mother if she'd seen anyone else who might be looking for Kieran lately. Have you seen any other strangers around this week?"

"Well ..." he hesitated, looking at his mother out of the side of his eye. "Maybe."

"Whatcha mean, *maybe*, son?" his mother asked, casting an eye over her shoulder.

Jasah's face paled a little, and Ekko could tell the boy knew something. Most likely, he'd been up to something which could land him in trouble, and he was afraid to tell them.

"Jasah, it's important that you talk to us," she began. She deftly climbed up on the gatepost and balanced herself on one foot, holding the other leg out at a right angle. She had the boy's rapt attention. "Sometimes we all do things we shouldn't, and we want to keep it a secret so we don't get in trouble. But some things are more important. We think your neighbor might be hurt, and that maybe some people came and hurt him. If you saw any other strangers around here, we'd really like to know. We might be able to find them and help Mr. Kieran." She met his eyes and then flipped backward off the post to land solidly on the ground.

Jasah's eyes dropped and he began tracing shapes in the dirt with his bare toe. "I might have come out to ... check on the chickens one night," he mumbled. "And then I might have heard some voices on the road speaking a language I didn't know. And *then*, I might have gone to take a look at them, but super quietly, so they wouldn't see me."

"And what did you see, lad?" asked Dalgis.

Jasah looked at this mother without raising his head, trying to gauge just how much punishment he'd be getting. But her face showed more concern than anger, giving him the courage to continue.

"I might have seen four people in dark cloaks on the road. Maybe dark blue, but it was hard to tell. They seemed to be arguing about something. One kept pointing toward town, and then one of the other ones kept pointing back the other way. I guess they were trying to decide which way to go. They ended up going back that way," he finished, pointing back down the road toward Kieran's cottage. "I hope they didn't hurt Mr. Kieran."

"I hope not, too," Daijera agreed, her voice soft and soothing. "Thank you for telling us the truth, Jasah. You are very brave." She reached over and patted the boy on the head, then turned and left the gated part of the yard. "Let's head back to the cottage and wait for the others," she whispered to Ekko and Dalgis.

"Farewell, young Jasah," called Dalgis. "May you grow to be wise and strong. Perhaps someday we shall meet again." Jasah moved to follow them, but his mother caught his arm.

Knowing that the remainder of the group would likely be gone for a couple more hours, Daijera volunteered to sort through the disaster of papers in the cottage, looking for anything that might be important or relevant to Kieran's abduction.

"I'll scout around to see if I can tell which way they went," Ekko offered.

Daijera raised her dark eyebrows. "You must be a very good tracker indeed, if you think you can find clues from something that happened a week ago." She paused, giving Ekko a chance to explain. When no explanation was forthcoming, Daijera gave her one more long look and went inside.

Dalgis made an attempt at lowering his voice. "Are you attempting to conceal the fact that you are a shifter?" he rumbled.

Ekko stared at him. "How did you know?"

"Because, child, you smell quite a lot like a fox. Daijera may not have scent receptors as keen as mine, but I do believe she knows that you are more than just a tiny human."

"Well, you're probably right about that, Dalgis, but I'd appreciate it if you didn't tell her anything. I prefer to keep my secrets to myself. I have learned not to be particularly trusting of people, and at the outside, I don't imagine we'll be in each other's company for more than another week. There's no reason for her to know."

"I don't think there's any harm in her knowing, Ekko, but I shall respect your wishes, of course."

"Thank you," she said, rather more curtly than she meant to. "I'm going to go *change* and see if I can catch a scent. Why don't you smell around as well, since your nose is so good? I'll check the woods and you can check back by the road."

"Capital plan," he agreed. "I'll meet you back here in ... well ... however long it takes."

She nodded and darted off into the woods to find herself a hollowed out log or similar place to stash her clothes while she scouted in fox form.

Argus

He could tell right away that something wasn't right about Kieran's house. The yard was overgrown, as it always was, but even before he reached the magical shielding of the wards, he could feel that the cottage was in distress. The absence of the tingly feeling he usually got when passing through the wards was deeply worrying. It took a minute for all the pieces to fall together, because as a father, he had the tendency to see everything at once and then sort out the details afterwards.

As he approached, he counted off the things that were wrong about the place. There were many tracks leading to the door, for one, and some of them were unusually large. Kieran had so few visitors that seeing the grassy pathway trampled flat was alarming all by itself. The door was open, but that wasn't necessarily unusual; it was the slightly skewed angle of the door that told Argus that one of the hinges had been torqued nearly to the point of being detached. And then there was the rustling. Someone was clearly inside, moving papers around from the sound of it.

Wary, he ducked behind an old wagon Kieran kept in front of the house despite having no horses to pull it. He edged around the back of it and closer to the window on the side of the main room. He peered in and saw something else that was atypical of Kieran, even in the best of times. The front room was neatly ordered, with four chairs tucked around the table and the sitting pillows tastefully arranged across from the door. On the sideboard opposite the window in which he was peering, Argus could see several stacks of neatly ordered papers weighed down with crystals so as not to fly away in the late morning breeze.

In all the years Argus had known Kieran, he had never known the man to be organized or concerned with the aesthetic arrangement of his home. He was a brilliant researcher into the mystic arts, to be sure, but he hadn't an artful bone in his body.

As he contemplated what to do, the source of the rustling became apparent. A shapely young woman with raven hair and a dancer's gait sauntered out of Kieran's study with another armful of papers and started sorting them into the stacks she had made on the sideboard. Is it possible Kieran had taken a wife? Not likely. From the look of this woman, Kieran was easily thirty years her senior and, while the man was brilliant, this woman with her tasteful, but expensive, traveling costume didn't look like the kind who would hitch herself to an old, ornery horse like Kieran.

Had he, perhaps, hired a housekeeper? Again, no. As a tavern owner, Argus knew what cleaning women looked like, and they *certainly* didn't look like this. And where was Kieran? The idea that he would allow some frou-frou female touch his papers, much less sort them, seemed like a complete impossibility. That realization settled Argus on the notion that this woman was, while perhaps not a thief exactly, up to no good.

As far as he was concerned, the direct approach was the best approach, so he quietly made his way along the wall until he was standing beside the broken door. On a mental count of three, he stepped very suddenly into the doorway, startling the woman and causing her to drop a handful of loose sheets.

"Who are you and what are you doing here?" Argus demanded.

The woman leapt backwards several feet, well outside Argus's reach and just far enough to give her maximum maneuverability in the small room. She made a quiet hissing sound and leaned back into a stance that conveyed to him that she had some training in hand-to-hand combat. Her elbow was slightly lower than was advisable for such a stance, however, and her hand positions looked more like she was prepared to claw him than use a highly-skilled melee attack. Not all that well-trained, then, but she looked like she might make up for some lack of skill with cleverness and sheer spirit.

"I might ask the same of you," she replied acidly.

"If you knew Kieran, you'd likely know me. You'd also know better than to touch his research. So I ask you again," he repeated with even more authority, "who are you, and what are you doing in Kieran's house?"

"You're right, I don't know him, or you. I'm looking for him."

"Are you now? And why is that?"

Her tone dripped sarcasm. "Why, to bring him a birthday present, naturally."

"Unlikely. He hasn't celebrated his birthday for at least a decade."

"As I said, I'm looking for him. That's all you get to know until I know who *you* are."

"No one to be trifled with," he snapped while making a quick gesture with his fingers. The stun spell hit the woman in the chest and, while she definitely felt its impact and staggered backwards, she didn't crumple to the floor as most people did.

She blinked her eyes hard and when she opened them again the irises were no longer human; she was staring at him with the slitted eyes of a serpent. If he had had any doubt about what she was, it dissipated when her lips drew back, revealing slightly elongated canine teeth.

Argus drew his sword. "What are you doing here, lamia? Where is Kieran?"

"Half-lamia, wizard. And I have no idea where he is. I told you I was looking for him. I thought your kind was better at recognizing when people were telling the truth.

Do you always attack random strangers who have presented no threat and spoken no lies?" Her back leg tightened, and he could tell she was preparing to spring. He also noticed moisture beginning to gather on her lips. Viper's Breath.

He'd heard of it and its effects, but as rare as lamias were, he'd never come in contact with it directly.

She was correct; wizards were generally very good at knowing when someone was trying to deceive them. Lying, unless one was extraordinarily skilled at it, caused slight shifts in a person's aura that any wizard worth his salt could spot. In his concern for Kieran, he had assumed that she was ill-intentioned. But her aura was strong and pulsing; she was angry and probably willing to kill him, but she wasn't lying about anything she'd said.

He realized that he might have acted in haste, but there was no undoing what had already been done. "I should think you might be able to appreciate how untoward this looks. Here you are, a total stranger, inside Kieran's house with the door broken in. You are going through his things, and now you're standing there ready to poison me when I didn't use any sort of lethal force."

"You're the one who attacked me, human."

"Well, well, who is this?" came a booming voice from outside. "Daijera, is this fellow with you?"

"Your timing is perfect, Dalgis," she called back. "This ... man ... and I are having a bit of a disagreement.

Argus wasn't sure who the booming voice belonged to, and he wasn't about to look, but he could tell it was someone *large*. The temptation to turn and face the newcomer was almost overwhelming, but Argus thought it best not to take his eye off the lamia. She raised one eyebrow, licked the poison droplets off her lips, and blinked. When her eyes re-opened, they were the same hazel-green eyes he'd seen when he'd first encountered her. She softened her stance, now confident that Argus couldn't get the advantage. She crossed her arms across her chest and smirked.

A large feathered head attached to a scaled neck snaked its way through the open window. "Well, now, I don't think there's any need for weapons here, friend. I'm sure we can discuss whatever is troubling you in a civil tone." Despite his annoyance at being outnumbered, Argus couldn't help but be charmed by the friendly nature of this beast.

"I came looking for my friend, Kieran," Argus explained, "and found this woman—Daijera, is it?—going through his things. I think my alarm was quite justified."

"Now, now," Dalgis soothed, "I believe we may all be on the same side here. We came looking for this Kieran fellow, and found his cottage ransacked. We have deduced that he's been abducted by some sketchy characters in dark robes. My friend Daijera here is looking for clues as to why he might have been taken."

"Why didn't she just say so, then?"

"Maybe because you were hurling stun spells at me," Daijera retorted.

Argus elected not to respond. "Why were you looking for him?" he asked Dalgis.

"We came to deliver a package from a friend of his, a chap named Zaos."

"Zaos Craxinna?" Argus asked.

"Indeed! Are you acquainted with him as well?"

"I am. We are part of the same research group."

"It seems I was correct, then," Dalgis smiled. "We do have a common goal. I think perhaps you ought to come with us when we return the package to Zaos."

Argus locked eyes with Dajera, whose jaw tensed at Dalgis's suggestion. This was going to be an interesting trip.

Dalgis

Within an hour, the group of three who had ventured into town seeking information returned with no clues, but several bags' worth of provisions and supplies.

Ekko returned to the house a few minutes later, and reported that she had had no luck in tracking anyone through the forest. This was no surprise to Dalgis, as he had concluded that the assailants, based on the faint, mixed scents he was able to follow, had returned to the road and headed back the way that he and his new friends had come the previous day.

All in all, Dalgis felt downright heroic, since he was the only one who had leads to follow.

For the first day, they simply followed the main road back toward Zaos's tower. Dalgis identified a game trail that ran generally parallel to the road, and it was this route that the kidnappers, if that's indeed what they were, seemed to have followed. It was a little bit exhausting for Dalgis, because his keen sense of smell had to be kept on high alert at all times, and he was terribly worried that he might miss something and let everyone down.

The following mid-day, he caught a whiff of the scent he identified as Kieran's (by far, his was the easiest to follow, as they had taken one of his spare outfits from the cottage and Dalgis could refresh his memory of the scent as needed) going off the game trail and deeper into the forest.

"Ho there, friends!" he called loud enough for the group to hear. " I seem to sense that our quarry went off the trail here!" He began slipping between the trees, following not only Kieran's scent, but the scents of four other humans. He reached a clearing that, based on the remains of a days-old fire circle, had been a campsite for the group they were seeking.

"Well done, Dalgis!" Ren affirmed. "They must have stayed the night here at some point. Let's all have a look around, shall we? Perhaps we'll get lucky, and they dropped something."

Dalgis didn't want to say anything until he was sure, but the scent of death assailed his nostrils. He cast a quick look over at Ekko, and she nodded gravely. She smelled it, too. Together they moved to the far edge of the clearing and followed the scent into the forest. Before they had gone thirty feet, they spotted an area where the angle of the earth rose and fell in ways unlike the surrounding forest floor.

Using his foreclaws, Dalgis began to dig very carefully while Ekko went to inform the rest of the party. By the time they joined him in the woods, Dalgis had uncovered what he knew to be the remains of the wizard Kieran.

"Where's his head?" asked Sora. "Please tell me it's in that hole somewhere."

"I'm afraid not, young lady," said Dalgis.

Sora shuddered and walked away. "I didn't bargain for this, Xezia," she muttered.

"No one ever bargains for a beheading," Dalgis retorted, as if she'd blamed him directly. She neither turned around nor stopped walking.

"She means," Xezia clarified, "that she didn't sign up to have to deal with necromancers. My guess is that our boy here knew something and wouldn't talk, and his captors got tired of keeping him alive with the risk of escape. They could take his head to a necromancer, who could, perhaps, compel him to give up information."

"Well, now, that's just disgusting."

"Sora would tend to concur with you, Dalgis. I hate to say it, but we should check his pockets. There might be something important that his attackers missed. Wizards often have secret pockets in their robes."

"Don't look at me, friend," Dalgis said, raising his arms. "Foreclaws are not good for fine movements."

"I'll do it," Ekko offered and dropped off of a low branch behind Xezia, startling him. "I'm not squeamish."

She scrambled down into the hole and began rifling through the soiled robes. After a moment, she re-emerged with a sour expression. "Nothing," she complained, "not even a single crown."

"Surely you hadn't been thinking to rob his corpse, Ekko!"

Ekko chuckled. "Aw, Dalgis, it's not like he has any use for money anymore."

"Well, I suppose you're right ... Anyhow, I do think we should re-bury him. There's no reason to take his body anywhere, and we can't just leave him out for the scavengers. In truth, he ought to be buried about twice as deeply as he was."

"That's very decent of you, Dalgis," murmured Argus, who had been silent throughout the entire discussion about his deceased friend.

"Oh, good heavens, Argus. I quite forgot he was a friend of yours. I'm terribly sorry we weren't able to find him alive."

Ren, who had also been quiet, stepped forward. "It may be no solace, Argus, but he was most certainly already dead by the time any of us arrived at his home. You could not have prevented his murder." Then he turned to the group. "I fear, though, that we must make haste in case we can prevent a second murder. I believe the odds are quite good that this band of killers is heading back to Zaos. We must try to come to his assistance."

"Quite right," added Xezia. "We should take a few moments to lay Kieran here to rest, but then we should get back to Zaos's tower as quickly as we can manage. We need to return to him in any event, so all that has changed is the speed at which we need to travel."

Chapter Six

Race to the Tower

Sora

There was really only one thing Sora hated more than elves who would betray their own kind and work for the likes of Ironshield and King Godfroy, and that was necromancers. Death wizards were abominations. They often claimed to worship Hoshkn, Goddess of Death, but they really violated everything She stood for. A very old woman who was a priestess of Hoshkn maintained a temple in Sora's childhood village, and the woman was very wise.

"Sora, it does not matter that you thought it would be prettier if it were colorful. You cannot paint things that are not yours, particularly not temple statues."

"But temples are public property," nine-year-old Sora reasoned. "The statue belongs as much to me as it does to Priestess Ralenn." Sora felt very clever, but her mother wasn't impressed.

"Don't give me that smart talk," her mother said. "You will scrub every speck of paint off that statue and you will assist the Priestess with any and all tasks she requires of you for the next moon cycle."

"An entire MONTH?" Sora wailed. "All I did was make Hoshkn look pretty!"

"You will learn respect, Sora. If not from me, then from the Priestess of Death."

When her mother said it like that, the prospect went from annoying and unfair to terrifying. Sora fell silent. She hoped her mother would think it was because she was angry, not because she was afraid.

The sun was high in the sky when they reached the temple, an open-air building with an elaborate series of garden beds. It was here that many members of the village were blessed and buried, their remains mingling with the soil and erupting into natural beauty of every shade and color. Sora's mother rang the bell that hung in a large circular gateway at the garden's entrance.

"Coming!" A shaky voice called from several flowerbeds away. It was several seconds before Ralenn came into view. She moved with the careful shuffling slowness of the aged, but her eyes were bright and cheerful. She was wrapped in an elaborate draped garment and wore an enormous hat on her head to protect her from the noontime sun. It was the first time Sora had seen her anywhere other than a festival, and the ancient lady's wide and welcoming grin seemed out of place on someone who worshipped the Goddess of Death.

When Ralenn finally reached the gate, Sora's mother bowed deeply. "My lady, my daughter comes to atone for what she did to the sacred statue. She will scrub it clean for you and serve you in any way you see fit for the next full moon cycle. We beg Hoshkn's forgiveness."

"Well, well," Ralenn mused, "isn't that lovely? Yes, I believe I can use her services. You show great respect by bringing her here. I shall keep her here until sundown, and then we shall negotiate what times she will come to assist me. This is good and right."

Sora's mother bowed deeply and bent down to look into her daughter's face. "Be good, listen, and learn. I will return for you at sundown." And then she walked away, leaving a confused and terrified child with a woman who seemed as old as time itself.

"Now then," the priestess began, "let us begin with the statue and make that our goal for today."

Sora nodded mutely and followed the old woman as she toddled toward a small house at the back of the garden. "Grab a bucket from the shed there and fill it at the water pump. Then return here. I will go and find you a scrub brush. You are lucky, I think, that the statue is made of marble and not a more porous stone." The old woman's face erupted into a thousand cracks when she smiled, and then she turned away to find the brush.

Sora did as she was told. She filled the water bucket, but as she struggled to carry it back to the house, she kept spilling so much that she had to go back and refill it. By the third time, she was nearly weeping in frustration.

"It's not necessary to always do things the hard way," came Ralenn's voice as Sora filled the bucket again. Sora turned to look at the old woman, who just smiled again and pointed to the shed where Sora had found the bucket. "Why don't you see if there's something in there that will make your task easier?"

It vaguely annoyed the child that this old-as-dirt priestess seemed to know how to solve the problem, and yet wouldn't just offer up the information. She stalked back into the shed and stood, hands on hips, looking around for something that would help her carry the water from the pump to the base of the statue. Her eyes finally fell on a small hand cart leaning upright against the wall. Would it work? It just might!

Awkwardly, she wheeled the cart out toward the water pump and lifted the bucket into it. She lifted the end of the cart slightly, then began to walk forward. While the water sloshed a little bit, she made it to the base of the statue without spilling more than a handful into the cart.

"Well done, child," said Ralenn, and Sora couldn't help but smile back as the pride welled within her. Ralenn extended her wiry arm and handed Sora a horsehair brush. "Here you go, dear. This should be sufficient to clean the paint off." She started to walk away, but then turned back. "Oh, and child, leave the shoes. I do believe Hoshkn would enjoy having purple shoes."

Over the course of the next month, Sora spent nearly every hour of daylight in the garden with Ralenn. She learned about how the bodies of the dead returned to the earth and nourished new life.

"Hohn and Hoshkn are not enemies, Sora, they are sisters. They love and respect each other, because their purposes are inextricably linked. There is no death without life, and no

life without death. One begets the other. It is the natural way of things. It is good and right."

"Good and right," Sora agreed.

"This is your last evening of service, child. I believe I shall let you choose the flowers for Hoshkn's offering tonight." Ralenn handed the delicate jeweled dagger to Sora. "You make the offering and your prayer. I shall thank the goddess for the gift of your company and service, but you may have a few words for her of your own today."

Sora's jaw hung open at the thought that such an honor would be hers. She took the knife carefully and walked around every flowerbed, finally deciding on a bluish hydrangea flower. She raised her hands carefully, as Ralenn had taught her to do. "Thank you, Hohn, for the life of this flower," she began. She had heard the words every evening, and now it was her honor to say them. She reached up and cut the flower's stem. "Thank you, Hoshkn. As I cut short the life of this flower, I bring its beauty into my memory, where it will live forever. Life and death, the great circle."

She held the flower gingerly in her hands and walked to the statue of Hoshkn that had brought her to this place what seemed a lifetime ago. She placed the flower on the still-purple shoes of the goddess.

"Thank you, Lady," she said. Then her eyes filled with tears and she couldn't find any more words. She was sure, though, that the goddess heard the words she could not find.

Yes, necromancers were abominations. They disregarded the sisterhood between Hohn and Hoshkn, and made a mockery of the delicate balance between life and death.

How had Xezia gotten her into this mess? When they met, he was examining the sea-going operations of Black Moon in order to better organize the humanitarian outreach arm of the criminal syndicate. Over the past year, though, he'd taken up more and more courier assignments, trekking back and forth across Rosend and dragging Sora along with him. He'd gone from negotiating delivery of supplies of medicine and food to being Allistair's errand boy. And now, what should have been a simple courier job was turning into a laundry list of her personal pet peeves.

The worst part of it was that she knew Xezia never did anything without thinking three steps ahead. Why hadn't they just swiped the package and taken it to Allistair, job done, payday cashed out? What was he up to?

Argus

The next day, Argus traveled with this strange cast of characters, observing them mostly in silence. He was fairly certain that Ren and Dalgis, whatever manner of beast he was, were on the level, but the rest of the party had (at best) questionable motives. It was possible that they all just wanted the ridiculous amount of crowns Zaos had promised them, but it seemed that there were other things at play here.

If they only knew what was in the package they carried, they would know that the 100 crowns each was a more than reasonable price to safeguard it. Argus suspected that he knew exactly what was in the chest: Zaos's research notebook which contained decades of research into the Holy Books—in particular, the Book of Order. Though many people believed the books to be nothing more than myths, the Scholars of the Six, a group of wizards dedicated to studying the earthly manifestations of the ancient gods, believed that the Books were not only real, they were scattered across the four kingdoms and hidden during the Heroes' War nearly a thousand years ago.

Argus's journey to Kieran's at the time of his kidnap and subsequent demise had been no accident. He had known that Kieran and Zaos both believed that they might be in danger, as both men had sent alarms through the portent bowls nearly two weeks ago.

Argus had been closing his inn tavern down for the night and settling the daily accounts in his office when the bowls began their melodic tones. He had looked up and watched as the viscous clear potion began to turn cloudy, like adding mud to water. He had been instantly concerned, and at first light he had turned the inn over to his wife and ten-year-old twins, instructing them to take good care of the business in his absence. He had hoped to return in two weeks.

Four hours' journey from his inn, there was a large library in the city of Windermere. The head librarian, another of the Scholars, was awaiting him when he walked through the doors.

She stood wringing her hands with worry. "Argus, I'm glad you're here. I was hoping you would have seen the portent and come right away. These signs can't be good."

"Signs?" Argus asked, raising his eyebrows. "I saw Kieran's bowl go cloudy a few hours before dawn. Has something else happened, Elspeth?"

"Yes," she replied, clutching her hands together even more tightly. The skin around her dark eyes puckered as she furrowed her brow. "This morning, Zaos's bowl also darkened. Can you believe it?" As wise as she was, she always looked just a little surprised when anything of interest, good or bad, happened in the world.

"Let me see the bowls."

She led him to her office in the back corner of the cartography section. Behind her desk, a long ebony shelf held six clear bowls, each bearing a unique sigil which denoted the identity of the mage. It was in every way identical to the ones behind his desk back in Breadstone. The liquid in two of them had turned gray and murky.

It was an imprecise system, but it was a foolproof way of communicating to the other Scholars when one felt one needed assistance. If the fluids turned green, it meant one of them had made a great discovery. Red communicated dire injury or illness. If a mage were to die, his or her liquid would turn black. The murky gray color signified that the mage feared mortal danger.

Elspeth was a small woman of the desert people, and her deeply bronzed skin hid her age most of the time, but her concern for her friends and colleagues betrayed her agelessness and made her look at once like a weary old woman and a frightened child. She paced the office aimlessly, unsure of what to do. She knew more about the gods than almost anyone alive, and could translate texts from eleven languages and countless dialects, but she was not a woman of action.

She drew back her crimson hood and let it fall around her shoulders, revealing a tangle of black hair untouched by gray or, it seemed, a comb. "You must go to them, Argus. I know it is a week's journey to Wheatfields, and I shall send my deepest apologies to your wife for detaining you. But you must help them, beginning with Kieran. Aerith may already be on the way, but you know how she is. If she is deep in her research, it may be days before she notices the portents."

Argus nodded. "I will head out within the hour," he agreed. "I'd like to write a message to my family, and I'd appreciate it if you'd see to it that it gets delivered."

That had been nine days ago.

Ren had been correct. There was no way Argus could have arrived in time to prevent Kieran's death, but these travelers had seen Zaos just a few days prior, so there was still reason to hope. Argus had no doubt that the attackers were headed toward Zaos, but the old man was craftier than people generally thought him to be. No doubt these people thought him a fool for paying such a price to send a package, but what they didn't know was that he had probably sent two or three other decoy packages within a small window of days. People always underestimated the cunning of the elderly, and Zaos had played the part they wanted him to play.

When they were only a small distance from the tower, the group paused to make a plan of approach.

"I think it might be wise," Dalgis suggested, "if young Ekko and I were to scout ahead. I can camouflage myself somewhat amidst the foliage and keep an eye on things, and Ekko can report back with the state of affairs."

Despite feeling pressure to hurry, even Argus agreed that the plan was far superior to charging forward with no foreknowledge of how things stood at the tower. When Dalgis disappeared into the woods with Ekko riding on his back, it was all Argus could do not to follow them, if only to make sure that they handled everything correctly.

The wait was excruciating. Sora sat on a large rock and used a stone from her bag to sharpen her sword. Xezia practiced a number of hand gestures, some of which Argus recognized as binding spells. Ren adjusted his armor. Daijera ... well, Daijera sat near Sora and played a light-hearted tune on something that looked like an ocarina. She was clearly talented as a musician, but as far as Argus was concerned, unlikely to be of any benefit to the party if fighting broke out.

After maybe half an hour, Ekko returned. “No one’s home. Same situation with the door blown off, unfortunately, but there was no scent of blood. I guess that’s a good thing. I didn’t investigate the inside of the place because I thought you’d all want to do that.” There was a slight fluctuation in her aura that Argus recognized as a half-truth, but he was far too concerned about getting to the tower to care about what she might not be saying.

“All right, then, no need for stealth,” Ren announced, though he was clearly shaken by the probability that the assailants had claimed his friend. “Let’s get moving.” He began walking down the road at a fairly rapid pace. Argus, who was a hair over six feet, had no trouble catching up with Ren, who was not only slightly shorter, but laden with armor. The two of them walked in common determination toward Zaos’s home.

Ekko’s report had been completely accurate. From a dozen yards away, it was clear that the door was similarly off its hinges. As they drew closer, Argus was able to take in every detail of the outside of the building nearly at once. On the left side of the manicured yard, an unusual mounded shape caught his attention.

“Dalgis? Is that you?”

Dalgis's head rose up from out of the hole he had dug. "Greetings, Argus. I am sorry to say that your friend is not at home. Let us hope that perhaps he had left before the miscreants arrived."

"Did you dig a hole ... in Zaos's lawn?"

"Indeed I did. It was immensely satisfying. The soil here is superb. I had a great deal of nervous energy as I was awaiting you, and now I feel almost completely calm."

"DO YOU HAVE ANY IDEA HOW MUCH MAGIC IT TAKES TO KEEP A LAWN LOOKING LIKE THIS?" Argus knew that the lawn, Zaos's pride and joy, was not the right thing to be focused on, but it was much easier to be angry about the treatment of his friend's yard than it was to give in to the fear he had for his friend's life.

"I'm dreadfully sorry, Argus," Dalgis answered, hanging his head. "I didn't really mean to damage anything. The grass just felt so nice ..."

Argus regretted his outburst, but all he managed to say was, "Please just fill in the hole as best you can. It would break the old man's heart if he were to come back to a Dalgis-sized trench in his lawn." Without waiting for a response, Argus walked through the broken door and headed directly for Zaos's research office on the second floor. He had to check ... maybe, just maybe ...

He pushed the door open, and though the room had been ransacked, just as Kieran's had been, the six bowls of liquid remained untouched on the shelf behind the desk. One had gone completely black. The other remained muddy.

The air whooshed out of Argus's lungs and he had to steady himself on the edge of the desk. Zaos was alive, and not gravely injured. Now that he knew that, he could focus on what the next steps were. He took a few more seconds to compose himself, then began searching through the debris of papers that covered the floor like a crinkly carpet.

Xezia

Having to navigate yet another person with yet another agenda was both frustrating and exhausting. Ren was already intractable, and it was clear that Argus was the same. Plus, they both actually knew these wizards, so there was no logical basis for Xezia taking the package from them. He had to figure out a way to get them to open the stupid thing so that he could see if it was the object of his mission or not.

When they arrived to find that Zaos had disappeared as well, Xezia saw an opportunity. Argus returned from wherever it was he had run to, and Xezia felt that this moment was probably his best chance at persuading the party.

"Well, Zaos is alive," Argus stated simply.

"That's excellent news," Xezia began. "I think it's clear that the package we've been asked to carry is the object of all these searches. Shouldn't we try to open the box to see what we're dealing with? Our lives may well be in danger because we are in possession of ... whatever it is."

"I'm fairly sure I know what it is," Argus replied.

"As am I," Ren chimed in.

"I feel as though you have the rest of us at a disadvantage, then, friend. We deserve to know what we're risking our lives to protect. We were told it was of no value to most people, and yet we have individuals who are clearly willing to kill for it."

Argus and Ren exchanged glances, and a silent understanding passed between them.

"I suspect it's one of Zao's research journals," Ren said, and Argus nodded. "I'm not sure it's wise to share much more than that, though."

"Wise for whom?" Xezia pushed. "Every one of us has put ourselves at risk, and now we have no one to return this box to, and we also only got half of our fees."

"Actually, we do have someone to return it to. We need to go to Swanford and take it to the librarian there. It's really the best option we have. She will have a safe way to store and study it. With any luck, we can find Zaos before these bastards kill him."

Xezia looked at Argus askance. "I didn't sign up for a rescue mission. I'm not saying we won't help. I'm just saying that wasn't on our agenda initially."

"Listen," Daijera cut in, "we should go through the debris here like we did at Kieran's. There might be something important, or a clue as to his whereabouts. We don't even technically know that he's been kidnapped."

"She's right," agreed Xezia. "We need to do a thorough search. Especially you two." He indicated Ren and Argus. "If the wizard left any clue behind as to his whereabouts, you are the ones who might recognize it."

He could tell Argus hated the idea of strangers pawing through his friend's belongings, but the logic was undeniable. Of course, finding Zaos wasn't really on Xezia's agenda, because what the Black Moon wanted was the book. But there might still be valuable information here. If they couldn't get their hands on the research journal, they might still be able to find clues that might lead to the Book of Order.

Additionally, if he could convince Argus to open the box and verify its contents, that might give him or Sora the opportunity to swipe the book and get back to Allistair. That would certainly earn him more favor than a collection of clues.

"Everyone spread out. Look for anything that appears to be deliberately well-hidden."

"Do you even see the irony in what you just said?" Ekko quipped.

"Something tells me that finding things which are supposed to be hidden is a specialty of yours," Xezia sneered back. He tried to sound dry and mildly acerbic, but the truth was that he rather admired her skills. She seemed to know her way around the shady side of the law, if her bulging pouch was any indication. He couldn't help noticing that all of the crystals Zaos had had on the table were no longer in their display boxes.

Ekko considered this, and apparently decided it wasn't an insult. She sprinted up to the second floor two steps at a time to search. Xezia was pretty sure a few more trinkets would find their way into her pouch.

In the meantime, he poked his head into Zaos's study and found it rather unremarkable for a man who was supposed to be one of the finest researchers in the realm. He performed an elaborate series of hand movements and then pressed his palms to his eyes. His vision darkened for a moment, but when it cleared, he scanned the modest room again. A faint glow seemed to be coming from one of the books in a pile at the base of the only bookshelf in the room. He reached into the pile and withdrew it. When he examined it more closely, he found that the book had a section cut out of the pages and a small bag of gold was tucked inside.

His spell had worked; it had found something hidden. But crowns weren't what he sought. He left the bag inside the fake volume and tossed it back into the mound. Seeing nothing else in this room, Xezia went back out into the main room where Daijera and Ren were searching through the disaster of Zaos's belongings.

There were no clear auras around any of the objects in this room, but the floor appeared almost misty somehow. He was confused. The charm he had cast should create a soft glow around any object that was hiding another one. There was no reason why the floor itself should appear to be covered in a thin layer of smoke, unless ...

Unless a more powerful magic user had taken the extra step to conceal the fact that something was hidden.

Xezia knew he was onto something. He began examining the floor foot by foot, beginning at one end of the room and moving across slowly. He investigated each floorboard in turn, moving one board at a time. Whatever was hidden here was clearly important, or Zaos wouldn't have gone to such trouble to mask it.

About halfway across the room, a small red rug with intricate golden patterns lay beneath an overturned end table. Xezia moved the table aside and set it upright, then lifted a corner of the rug so that he could inspect the boards underneath.

But the rug did not lift. It was affixed to the ground in an unusual fashion.

"Can someone assist me with this?" he called. Naturally, Sora was at his side in less than a second. Together, they began working on the rug, trying to lift it from the floor. Sora pulled her sword out of its sheath and tried to slide it underneath, but could only insert it a couple of inches. She readjusted so that she was driving her sword between the boards at the edge of the rug, but the blade seemed to hit solid stone after being inserted an inch deep.

"I have an idea," Xezia said, and pulled an iron dagger out of his boot. Magic didn't particularly like iron and, while there was nothing special about this blade otherwise, it was certainly worth a try. He tried inserting it between the floorboards as Sora had tried to do, and as the blade slid into the same spot hers had occupied, there was a *pop* of light that surprised him and knocked him backwards onto his rear.

Sora chuckled, and at first Xezia was annoyed, but when he looked back at the rug, he could now see a faint outline around the edges. "HA!" he cried, knowing he had found what he sought, even though he wasn't quite sure what that was yet.

His exclamation attracted Argus's, Daijera's and Ren's attention, and all came over to try their hand at moving the rug.

After a moment, Argus stated aloud what they all knew. "There's a hatch here that's magically sealed."

"I don't suppose you know how to open it?" Xexia asked hopefully, but with the slightest bit of sarcasm lacing his words.

Argus turned a stern eye on the smaller man. "I am pretty sure I'm the only one here who CAN open it. He's probably put a Scholar's Lock spell on it. That also probably means he doesn't want anyone other than a Scholar in there."

"I'm fairly certain he also doesn't want to be kidnapped and killed."

Argus did not reply, but set his jaw and walked into the smaller study, returning a moment later with a jar of coppery powder and a small funnel. He drew an elaborate sigil on the carpet by feeding the powder through the funnel, then fished a flint out of his pocket and lit it. The symbol leapt to life with green fire and then burned out within seconds. The green glow of the fire spread to the edges of the rug and then sputtered out. Argus reached down with one hand and easily lifted the trap door, revealing a ladder leading to a dark room below.

"Let me go find a torch," Ren offered, but Xezia was already climbing down the ladder.

"Feel free to join me once you do," he smirked. "I see fairly well in darkness." He knew the spell he cast would faintly illuminate the room, for another fifteen minutes at least, and he wanted to be the first to examine the contents of the hidden basement.

The ladder was nearly nine feet, and then Xezia found himself standing in a relatively small chamber, perhaps ten feet square. The walls were lined with metal sheets.

Unlike the messy room upstairs, this one was meticulously organized. Vials, bottles, and pouches, all clearly labeled, were precisely arranged on shelves along one of the walls. Another wall was lined with bookcases, all filled with leather-bound tomes, folios, scrolls, even boxes of what appeared to be letters. There was a six-foot-long table in the center of the room opposite the ladder, laden with a variety of tools: mortar and pestle, inks and quills, magnifying lenses, candles, and scales. At the farthest end of the table, a book lay open with a half-inscribed parchment snugly fit in the crease.

As Xezia began to examine the book, he heard Argus's heavy footsteps descending the ladder. He looked closely at the parchment and saw that it held symbols he didn't recognize.

That was a rare thing for Xezia, as he spoke six of the nine living languages of the realm with fair skill, and could recognize the lettering of the other three, even if he couldn't not understand them.

One side of the parchment was written in Dyosa, the most widely-spoken language in the four kingdoms. Arrows drawn to the other side connect the Dyosa letters to strange and foreign symbols. Zaos had clearly been working on creating something akin to an alphabet key for this new language. Was he creating a code, or was it something else?

Chapter Seven

The Spoils of Battle

Elia

She awoke to the smell of burnt flesh.

It took her a moment to orient herself. Where was she? What was this weight crushing down on her? Why wouldn't her limbs move? As the world came into focus, Elia became aware of the horror of her situation. The memories of the past day came back to her in a flood.

The battle had been a brutal one, even by Ironshield's standards, and it had been the first time she had seen the front lines. Up to now, she had worked only in the healing tents, using her expertise in herbal remedies and poultices to prevent infections in the wounded. But then General Dol had sent for her.

She had finished stitching and wrapping a wound on a young soldier and then reported directly to the General's tent. She stood just inside, next to the guards, unsure how to announce her presence as the General and a woman in imposing black armor huddled over his desk, murmuring quietly. After a moment, Elia cleared her throat uncertainly, and the grizzled military leader looked up from his war map.

"Ah, you must be the healer girl."

"Uh, yessir. I mean no, sir."

General Dol rubbed his beard and sighed in exasperation and exhaustion. "Which is it, child?"

The woman in black stared at Elia with threatening intensity.

"Well, sir, it's sort of both," Elia forced herself to focus on the General and ignore the woman. "I am working in the healing tent, but I have no healing magic to speak of. I'm just an herbalist."

"I was told that you had some skill in magic," he grumbled. The battle wasn't going very well for Ironshield, and the losses were taking their toll on the general.

"I ... I'm not sure what you're looking for, sir. I do have some psychic abilities, but I'm no battle wizard. To be completely honest, sir, I know I was conscripted, but I would make a terrible soldier. I don't think I could bring myself to kill someone who hadn't wronged me."

"You have no idea what these savages are capable of, child. But as it happens, we don't need you to fight. We have several battle wizards, but they seem to be less effective against these creatures than we would have expected. We need to change our strategy. Do you have any skill in protective magic?"

"Like wards and things? Yessir."

"How long do you think you could hold protective shielding over our troops?" Dol asked.

"I ... don't know, sir. Several minutes, I should think, provided I could concentrate and wasn't being attacked myself." Protection? That might be something she could do. One could not refuse conscription into the Ironshield military; the penalty was death if you refused to serve. And while she didn't see any reason why King Godfroy needed to take over the region on the Ironshield's border with Heavenly Skies, she didn't like the idea of public execution either. She had volunteered for medical duty as a way to keep herself busy caring for the injured instead of fighting, but it didn't work for very long.

The woman whispered something in his ear, and the General nodded. "Several minutes is good. You can provide magical cover from behind the fighting lines, allowing our troops to advance and engage hand-to-hand. Humans are larger and stronger than most of the fighting force we're seeing from Heavenly Skies. I think if we can move in on them, we have a much better chance of taking this section of the border."

"I ... I definitely would prefer to protect people than kill people, sir. But I wouldn't be able to be too far away. I think I'd need to be within a hundred feet or so to cast any reliable protection. Maybe even closer."

"Not to worry. You'll be behind some of the finest fighters we have. The Heavenly Skies army won't get anywhere near you."

He hadn't been wrong, but ultimately, it hadn't mattered. Ironshield had gravely underestimated the capabilities of the non-human army. Elia had been able to shield the human troops from rains of arrows using an umbrella of light energy, but after the first volley of arrows clattered helplessly to the ground, Heavenly Skies had wheeled out an enormous beast on a cart. It rather resembled a three-eyed mudpile the size of four horses together, and had brown and orange mottled skin. Fear-induced adrenaline coursed through Elia's veins as she recognized the beast as a lava toad. She had watched helplessly as the creature opened its gaping toothless mouth and seemed to swallow the sunlight. She had looked on in horror as it then belched out five flaming projectiles which sailed in graceful, glowing arcs toward the Ironshield army.

The balls of light hit Elia's shield and actually sucked in its energy as they passed through it. Then they hit the earth with such force that dozens of soldiers were blown backwards, their bodies burning and becoming an exponentially larger grouping of fire bombs.

There was no time to run, though Elia did stumble back a few feet as a wave of flaming bodies flew toward her position. The troops in front of her began screaming in terror, and while Elia's vision was transfixed by the fiery scene playing out before her, hundreds of soldiers fled, trampling each other in an attempt to get out of range. By the time she realized what was happening, Elia was caught up in the wave of panicking men and women.

It was everyone for him or herself, and Elia could not withstand the onslaught. She felt herself getting pushed down, like she was a calf caught in a stampede. She covered her head as best she could, but she was unable to get away as she saw the armored boots running toward her. They were the last things she saw before she lost consciousness.

She had no idea how long ago that had been, but based on the lack of battle sounds, it was a good while. Elia opened her eyes and the acrid stench made them burn and water. As her surroundings came into focus, she found herself trying to scream, but only squeaky breath came out.

She was lying more or less on her side and all she could see were limbs ... charred, bleeding, *dead* limbs. After she had been knocked out, there must have been another volley of blasts from the lava toad, and her unconscious form had been buried under the flying bodies. The irony that it was the corpses on top of her that probably saved her life was lost in her panic and desperation to escape.

Elia found that she was able to move her head, so she searched for a possible escape route, and she found one to her right shoulder. She struggled to free her arms and forced her way onto her stomach so she could crawl out. As she inched forward, the carnage pile settled, pushing the air from her lungs in a pained cry. She began sobbing, but refused to yield to the rising fears.

Her legs were pinned under the weight of the fallen soldiers, so she dug her nails into the scorched and gory earth and pulled herself forward for what seemed like an eternity. She kept her eyes focused on the sliver of light that meant the end of her entrapment. She had moved maybe ten inches when the pile settled again, but this time, the weight shift worked in her favor. Her left leg was free!

With a weeping grunt, she pushed with her leg and pulled with her arms, and she began closing the distance. *Just a little farther. Almost there.* She forced herself to focus only on the shard of sunlight. Finally, her arms cleared the opening and she could feel the warmth of the sun. With renewed energy and a desperate scream of exertion, she pulled her torso out from under the heap.

Once her body was fully free, she tested her strength to see if she could stand. Nothing appeared broken, though she had splotchy red burns on her arms where smoldering flesh had rested against her for no-one-knew-how-long. Everything was sore and covered in filth, but functional.

Suddenly, it occurred to her that troops from Heavenly Skies might be searching the battlefield for survivors to finish off or take prisoner. She crouched down and surveyed the landscape, but saw no such threat. Instead, her eyes took in the grisly truth ... the battle had ended hours, maybe days, ago, and the field was littered with bodies, mostly those of the army she had been trying to shield.

The smell was not as bad as it had been underneath the dead soldiers, but the horror before her was more than her mind could take. Her breaths came more and more quickly, and her heart thudded against her ribs. Suddenly, her abdomen seized and she fell to her knees, spewing sick all over the scorched grass. When there was nothing left inside of her, she fell to her side and wept.

At some point in her weeping, Elia fell into a deep sleep, fraught with disturbing dreams.

Shadows of judges in gray robes both danced and fought with motley-clad court jesters. The jesters erupted into lunatic laughter while the judges told them to quiet themselves. And above it all, Elia sat in a chair far too large for her, as though she were a toddler sitting in her father's seat at the table. Suddenly, the judges and jesters all looked up at her and fell silent.

Elia woke with a start, and by the position of the sun, she judged it to be a couple of hours before sunset. Despite still being traumatized and shaky, she made a decision as she lay on the grass, staring at the sky.

No more.

She had never wanted to be part of this war.

She had been left for dead on the battlefield, and as far as she was concerned, she would stay dead. If she returned home, she would be forced back into service, or labeled a traitor and deserter. No one would believe that she had survived under a mound of fallen bodies. She would go somewhere where Ironshield was not waging war. Somewhere no one would know her.

She would flee to Benedictus. From what she had heard, there were people of all races there, living their lives away from King Godfroy's genocidal hatred. If she followed the setting sun, eventually she would reach the sea. There, she would find a way to pay for passage to Benedictus and away from this life.

She looked down at her bloody and sooty robes. She stripped down to her chemise and, steeling herself to do what she must in order to survive, she located a soldier of similar size. He looked to be a boy of no more than fourteen, younger even than she was, his life, potential, and future cut viciously short. Tears stung her eyes, but she knew she couldn't afford to *feel* until she was far, far from this place of misery and blood. She put her agony in a box in her mind and locked the lid tight, then she reached down and claimed the boy's trousers, which were in fair shape. She also scavenged a short sword and sheath on a belt, a dagger, a purple traveling cloak, and two canteens. She used the water from one to rinse her face and hands. She must still look a sight, but at least now she didn't look as obviously fresh from battle.

She scavenged a few more items from the soldiers and then said a prayer for their souls and their forgiveness at her thievery. She wasn't even certain to which Deity she aimed her prayer. Perhaps just to the restless dead around her.

Heading toward the thickest part of the forest to the west, she sobbed as she walked, knowing she would never see her family, friends, or beloved village of Breadstone again.

Ekko

This was literally the most disappointing burglary experience of her life. No one bothered to be suspicious that she'd gone upstairs alone. The room had already been tossed, which made finding anything interesting exceedingly difficult. Everyone downstairs basically left her alone, so she didn't even have the thrill of trying not to be discovered.

And maybe worst of all, this man had nothing in the world she wanted to swipe. No jewelry, no art. Not even a silver comb. Even the books the wizard had up in his sleeping quarters were useless. She had looked through most of them, and they were *boring*. Ledgers of his purchases, genealogy charts for the royal families of the Four Kingdoms. Sketches of local plants and animals signed by someone named Dorset. Not even a well-known artist. *Ugh.* She snagged a richly leatherbound book of royal histories that might fetch a price somewhere with history-focused book collectors, but on the main, she considered this a complete waste.

She decided to move on to the closet, hoping she'd find something more exciting than Zaos's robes and underclothes. And though it didn't scratch her thieving itch, she did find something interesting.

In the back of the closet, the clothes appeared to be somewhat damp. Suspicious and intrigued, Ekko moved slowly and raised her hand to feel the air. As she suspected, there was the slightest breeze brushing along the edges of the few clothes that were still hanging.

She'd broken into a noble's home once (not to steal anything really, just to see if she could do it) and found something similar: a secret door built flush with the walls. As her fingers felt along the corner, moving air tickled her fingertips. She traced the wall down to the bottom corner, where she found a small hole, just big enough for a finger. She hooked her index finger into the hole, and when she pulled, the entire panel fell free, revealing a space maybe three feet square with a ladder going up to the roof. The trap door to the roof was wide open, allowing the morning dew to make its way inside.

She scrambled up the ladder and poked her head out of the opening. There, hidden from being seen from the ground by the slight peaks in the roof, was a flat section covered in elaborate symbols painted on the ground. This was definitely *not* her area of expertise. After a moment's deliberation, she descended and went to fetch someone who might know what to make of what she found.

That somebody was probably the new guy, Argus.

She stood at the top of the stairs, and was surprised to see that the room was empty. "Hello?" she called.

"They've all gone down to the basement, Ekko," Dalgis said, somewhat glumly. His head and neck were lying in the entryway, since his body wouldn't fit through the door. He sighed heavily, clearly sad to be left out of all the adventure.

Ekko spotted the trap door in the floor. She trotted down the stairs and poked her head down into the hole.

"Um, I think there's something up here Argus needs to see."

The wizard, having heard her call, ascended from the cellar and followed her back up to where she'd found the secret ladder. Argus began to climb and Ekko followed him.

There was a great circle on the flat space on the roof, inlaid into the floor with shiny stones. The circle was divided into quarters by straight lines which seemed to align with the cardinal directions, and each quarter contained a variety of symbols, also inlaid. At each of places where the dividing lines intersected the circle, someone had placed candles of different colors. All the candles had melted entirely, leaving only misshapen puddles of wax.

Argus examined all of this with a grim expression. Then he made a hand gesture and there was a small flash of light. He nodded, satisfied, then said, "Let's go downstairs and I'll tell everyone about this at the same time. It puts a very different spin on things."

Back in the main room, Argus explained what he had seen on the roof above. Everyone listened intently, waiting for his explanation, except for Xezia, who was nodding as if he had already figured out what Argus was going to say.

"It's a travel spell," Xezia announced, as though he had been the one to make the discovery.

"It is indeed," continued Argus, unfazed. "What we cannot tell from the circle is whether Zaos cast it himself to leave the premises or whether someone else cast it and took him away."

Dalgis's head came up from the floor. "There's no blood smell here; that's a most excellent sign!" He seemed very pleased to be able to offer useful information, and Ekko patted him and smoothed his feathers.

"That is a good sign, probably," Argus agreed, "but we are still in a bit of a quandary. We have no way of knowing where he went, only that he is alive and still believes himself to be in danger. He could have traveled to Galantus with that spell, or someone could have taken him straight to King Godfroy. We have no way to know."

"Why would King Godfroy want him?" Xezia asked, and it seemed to Ekko that his tone was that of a man who knew the answer to a question and was testing you to see if you'd lie.

Argus looked at each member of the group in turn, and then seemed to make a decision. "Zaos is one of the greatest researchers in our generation, and he's been studying the old stories of the Holy Books."

"Those are children's stories," Daijera stated. "Are you trying to tell us otherwise?"

"I'm not telling you anything conclusively. But Zaos believed the Books in the stories were, like nearly all myths, based in some sort of truth. The Books might not be divine-level spellbooks, as the stories would have us believe, but Zaos believed he was quite close to discovering the location of the Book of Utrui, the Book of Order."

"Do you think he found it?" asked Ren. "Is there any chance that we've been toting a Holy Book all over the south of Rosend?"

"Not likely," Argus replied. "I suspect that the chest contains Zaos's research, and he was sending it to Kieran, so Kieran could take it to the librarian Aerith in Swanford."

"Then that's where we must take it at once!" cried Dalgis. "We mustn't lose any more time. Wait ... you mentioned King Godfroy. Why would Godfroy have an interest in such things?"

"Because he also believes the Books are real, but he believes that they are, in fact, divine grimoires. He believes that if he can possess them all, his armies will be unstoppable and he will be able to wipe all races other than humans out of the Four Kingdoms, allowing him to make them all human kingdoms under his supreme rule."

The silence in the room spoke volumes. Finally, Xezia spoke. "How do you know this?"

"Because I'm a wizard from Ironshield, and Godfroy is far too arrogant to be secretive about his plans. He believes the excitement of the quest will inspire wizards and mages to follow him. Let me be clear about something. If these Books do exist, no matter what their actual contents are, it is imperative that the Blood King never gets his hands on them."

They all murmured agreement.

"I guess we'd all better get a good night's sleep, then," Ekko sighed. "It's a three-day trek to Swanford from here. I just hope this Aerith person is willing to pay us the remainder of our fee."

Xezia

The afternoon had been a very productive one. Not only had Xezia learned the probable contents of the package, confirming Allistair's suspicions, but he was also fairly certain he'd learned how Allistair had gotten his information. If Godfroy was making it public within Ironshield that he was seeking the books, one of the Black Moon wizards in that country had undoubtedly sent word to Allistair.

Xezia wasn't sure why that irritated him, but it did. He pulled Sora aside as the party was setting up to stay the night in Zaos's tower, with the plan being to head for Swanford after a good night's rest in a safe location. Such luxuries should not be passed up, Daijera had argued, and in the end, everyone agreed.

"Allistair made it sound like it was his reputation and eminence within Black Moon that earned him this intelligence," Xezia complained, "and it turns out that the information is common knowledge in Ironshield."

Sora chuckled. "You just don't like feeling like someone's put one over on you," she smiled. "Of course Allistair is going to build up his role in gathering the information.

Reputation is everything at his level of the organization. The ability to influence people and governments and having knowledge other people don't is literally the only thing that allows him to maintain his position. What do you think would happen if people knew that most of the information he hoards so carefully isn't secret at all in other parts of the world?"

"You have a point," he replied, and for a moment, the energy between them was like it had been a year ago, like they were partners in crime, in on a joke no one else understood. Over the past year, he had started hiding his ever-darkening thoughts from her, afraid that she would judge him for them or be frightened by them, ultimately abandoning him at her first opportunity. But even as things had become more strained, he had come to rely on her companionship and leveling presence. He wondered if she knew that, and that that's why she hadn't left, blood debt or no.

"The question is, what do we do with this information? Are you going to try and send word to Allistair, or should we swipe the chest and try to find someone who can open it?"

"I think it might be wise to stick with this party for a little while longer. I'm going to try and convince Argus to open the chest, which I'm sure he can. I have an idea ..."

Sora snorted. "I don't like that look, Xezia. When you get that look, it means you're thinking of doing something reckless that might get us killed."

"Well, then you'd be absolved of your debt to me, wouldn't you?" He immediately regretted the harshness of his statement. Not only had he revealed his own fears, he had also ruined the moment. Her face clouded over and she leaned back, crossing her arms across her chest.

"I guess there is that," she replied coolly. "What's your idea?"

"It's a solid one, and we can back out of it easily if it looks like it will fail," he said, trying to regain her goodwill, but she remained stoic. "If I can convince Argus to open the chest, and the book inside does, in fact, lead to Utrui's Book, then we can stay with the group long enough to use the benefit of numbers to get our hands on THAT Book. Now THAT would give us some real pull in Black Moon. Allistair would have to give us whatever we want for it, and we'd start being the ones with the powerful reputation."

"And what would you do with that? All that recognition?"

"I could position myself to be more respected within the organization, as could you. You could take only jobs you want to take. No more having to take on smuggling runs for poisoners or slavers, just because Black Moon orders you to." He knew her soft spots, and he wasn't trying to manipulate her with them, not really. He just needed her to stay.

She thought about this for a moment, then nodded. "You could be onto something there. See if you can convince Argus. If you can, then we go with your plan. If not, we steal the book and take it to Allistair. Deal?"

"Deal."

Trying to convince Argus to open the package and investigate the contents was downright anticlimactic. When Xezia went to the study to speak to him, he found Argus standing by the desk, mumbling an incantation, and making tiny, intricate movements with his fingers. Xezia remained prudently silent until there was a tell-tale crackling, like tiny lightning, in the air. Argus dropped his arms and sighed deeply. As he reached up to mop his brow with his sleeve, Xezia cleared his throat.

"Ah, Xezia. I was just thinking that we really need to verify that the contents of this box are what we think they are."

"I couldn't agree more. In fact, I was just coming here to discuss it with you. Shall we?"

Argus nodded. Xezia kept a genial tone, but he was fairly certain that, had he not walked up when he did, Argus would have kept the information he discovered to himself. Everyone liked to hoard their own secrets.

As it was, though, Argus made no attempt to conceal the book or its pages. He allowed Xezia to look on as he flipped through the dog-eared pages. There were a few diagrams and non-specific maps, but the writing inside appeared to be little more than gibberish.

"Of course, he encoded it," Argus sighed.

"Can you decrypt it?"

"Not without some sort of notes or key or something. Zaos was a master at codes and ciphers."

"Ciphers, you say?" Xezia asked, perking up. "Hold on." He leaned his head out the doorway and spotted Daijera spreading a blanket on the chair where she intended to sleep. "Daijera, do you have that cipher key you found at Kieran's?"

"Of course," she grinned. She gave Xezia a wink, perhaps to congratulate him on making progress on his mission. She fished in her backpack and brought him the small journal.

"Try this, Argus," Xezia suggested, holding out the book. "We found it at Kieran's before you joined us."

Argus opened it up and laid it next to the larger book. "Yes ... this goes with ... right ... okay, that makes sense ..." He was clearly lost in the decoding, and anticipating what came next, Daijera fished paper, a pen, and an ink pot out of the desk drawer and laid it silently next to Argus's right hand. Then she winked at Xezia again and slipped out of the room, leaving him to "assist" Argus with the decoding process.

They worked for two hours, each translating separate pages and numbering them carefully. It became apparent almost immediately that this research was entirely devoted to the Book of Order. The first section of the book appeared to be dedicated mostly to lore and information about Utrui as a Deity.

"...and, lo, there was Utrui, Lord of Order, who stood against the madness of the wild hoards ... and he gave them Law, and the ways of governance, that they might rise from Chaos ... and Rahmgn, bringer of Chaos, raged against his brother; but alas, it was too late. Reason now lived in the hearts and minds of those who were capable of understanding Utrui's words ... and the wild edges of the world were left to Rahmgn to reign over, and yet he was unsatisfied ... so began the struggle between brothers..."

None of it was particularly revelatory, but it spoke of Deities who were intricately involved in the affairs of society, and in the hearts of those who lived there. It wasn't uncommon to see stories of Epi this way; in fact, that was one reason Xezia had chosen her to follow. In his heart, he hoped and believed she would hear him when he prayed. Every child heard the story of how Utrui had reached into the mind of the leaders of each tribe of people and re-organized their minds so they could perceive him, but he had never heard of Utrui being described as *fighting* for the hearts of people.

The night was wearing on and the candle had nearly burnt down to the end of its wick. Argus yawned mightily. “I think we should put these notes in order, and then perhaps keep working on the journey. It would be enormously helpful to Aerith if we had managed to translate most of it.”

“Should we not split up the pages between us, just in case we are intercepted somehow?”

Argus looked at Xezia with new appreciation. “Yes, in fact, I think that’s an excellent idea. You take the odd-numbered pages, and I’ll take the even ones.”

Xezia smiled. “I’m glad you’re in agreement. I do think this will be safer.”

A very productive day indeed.

Chapter Eight

A Clandestine Meeting

Ren

Under normal conditions, Ren considered himself a patient man. But now, traveling back along the road they had already traveled twice—first north, then south, now north again—Ren found himself feeling rather peevish at all this back-and-forthing. Why, he wondered, had Argus and Xezia thought it was their right to open Zaos's package and start going through its contents? And why was it necessary to deliver this book to the Swanford librarian? Why would it be safer there? Shouldn't they be trying to find Zaos instead?

All this walking was dull and frustrating, and it gave him far too much time to think. Ren was a man of action, and walking, well, walking wasn't much of an action. He said as much to Dalgis.

"Ah, I can quite sympathize, Sir Ren," Dalgis said kindly, "but in truth, we have no way to go looking for your friend, as we have no clues as to where he has gone. I believe Argus is of a similar mind, and this quest to bring the book to this librarian is all he can think to do."

"You may be right, Dalgis," Ren admitted. "You are quite wise. I just wish I felt like we were accomplishing something."

"Safeguarding your friend's research does accomplish something, does it not?"

"I suppose it does. But it doesn't FEEL like something."

"Perhaps we shall be fortunate, and Zaos will have transported himself to Aerith, and he will be there waiting for us!"

Dalgis's good humor was hard to deny, and Ren found himself wanting to believe this fantasy, though he knew the odds in its favor were astronomical. It did make him feel a little better, though, so he allowed the tiniest flame of hope to glow in his heart. It made the walk more pleasant.

Swanford was a rather large town, and they arrived just after sunset. They found an inn that could accommodate them which also had a very nice stable for Dalgis. They sat at a large table in the common room of the inn and, thanks to a generous payment to the innkeeper by Ekko, they were enjoying the largest meal they'd eaten since they'd met.

"I'm telling you, Argus," Xezia was saying as he chewed on a bite of pheasant, "this is a momentous discovery. If he's right, then there actually is a physical Book, and if Ironshield were to get these notes, they could find it. Do you really think it's a good idea to give the translation to some doddering old woman? I mean no disrespect, but I find it unlikely that she could guard it sufficiently."

"I want to disagree with you, but I have doubts as well. Aerith is very wise and a powerful mage, but I fear that she has the wrong temperament to defend something that would be so valuable to Godfroy."

"Just what are you proposing?" Ren asked. He still didn't trust Xezia, though the man had been nothing but true for the entirety of their acquaintance.

"I think," Daijera said, almost as though she were talking to herself, "that he's proposing that we give the journal to Aerith and then try to find the Book of Order ourselves."

"We?" Argus and Ren said at once.

"Certainly. I can't speak for anyone else, but I'm having some good fun. I do travel a great deal, but just to perform for some noble family here or establishment- on-contract there. This is my first quest, and I'm having a wonderful time. I think Dalgis is, too."

"I just want to get paid," added Ekko, mouth full of pheasant. "A quest might mean treasure. Treasure means getting paid BIG."

Daijera

After most of the party had turned in for the night, Daijera slipped out of her window and made her way over to the stable. She poked her head in the sliding door and spotted Dalgis in a cloud of flying hay.

"Dalgis," she laughed, "what in the world are you doing?"

"This hay itches," he complained. "I don't know how horses stand it. The entire stall is lined with the stuff, and I just can't get comfortable."

"Let me help." Daijera set down the bundle she was carrying and grabbed one of the brooms from the stable-hand's tool stand. Dalgis stepped out of his stall, and she swept all the hay into a large pile just outside the stall gate. "There you go."

"You cannot possibly imagine how much I appreciate that. I really do like the stable accommodations. It's just that blasted hay."

"I brought you something else, my friend," she smiled, and reached for the bundle she had brought out. "Close your eyes."

"Oooh, a surprise! I do love surprises! At least I think I do. I'm not sure I've ever had one before."

She laid her gift on the floor of the stall. "Okay, open."

He opened his eyes to find two very fluffy pillows on the ground. His jaw hung open.

"Goose down, just for you. A little nest for your head."

"I am gobsmacked, kind lady." He flopped down on his side and laid his enormous head on the pillow. "Ahhhh ..."

"Have a good night's sleep, Dalgis." If he replied, she didn't hear it.

Instead of returning to her room, she slipped out behind the stable and into the alley. Her destination was about a half mile away, and she didn't have time to waste. She didn't expect any of the party would come to her room looking for her, but it was better not to take chances.

The orphanage was tucked away against the city wall, or so it appeared. She swung herself over the low wall and crossed the outdoor play pitch to the gardening shed at the rear. The shed appeared to be a six-by-eight foot structure leaning against the exterior wall of Swanford, but the intricate door knob shaped like a flaming sun revealed its true identity.

She knocked twice, swiped her hand across the door, then knocked again. Immediately, the door swung inward and a gnomish woman stood in the dark opening with her hands on her hips.

"Show me yer ticket."

Daijera bent down and pulled her hair back. The gnome reached up and folded up the lobe of Daijera's ear, revealing a tiny tattoo of a black moon (which, to be honest, looked more like a splotch of black ink). Satisfied that Daijera was safe to enter, she let go of her ear and let her stand back up.

"State yer bizniss," she hissed.

"I'm looking for Shar," Daijera whispered back.

"Follah me."

Daijera slid through the opening and closed the shed door behind her.

At first glance, it looked like a typical garden shed, the area littered with a wheelbarrow and various tools, bags of seeds, a chair where the gnome had apparently been sitting, and a table for potting small plants which was set against the wall. The gnome walked over to the potting table and reached behind one of the legs. Daijera heard a *click*, and the wall behind the table (and the table itself, which had been cleverly affixed to the wall) swung open, revealing a set of descending stairs.

"The ketch is right here when yer ready to leave." The gnome pointed at a brass ring attached to the inside of the secret door.

"Thanks," Daijera replied and started down the dark and narrow stairway. There was a dim glow at the bottom which provided just enough light for her to see the stone steps in front of her. At the bottom of the stairs, a short hallway curved to the left, with a door on each side and a door at the end. She stepped up to the first door on the left and repeated the secret knock. The door opened, and she found Sora there, grinning at her.

"About time you got here!" she chuckled.

"You guys must have left right after dinner. I waited awhile, just to make sure everyone was settled in."

"Ah, Daijera," said a new voice. A tall elven woman with silvery hair and eyes the color of the deep sea rose from behind a desk and extended her hand. Daijera placed her hand palm-to-palm with the other woman in the traditional sea elf greeting. "Happily met."

"Happily met, Shar."

"Every day of my life," Shar laughed. "Good to see you again, Daijera. Been about two years, eh?"

Xezia rose from a chair next to the desk. "Nice to finally be able to speak freely," he said.

"Xezia has just been updating me on your progress in acquiring the Craxinna package. Do you concur with his assessment that it would be best to continue to follow and monitor this party rather than extract the book and yourselves immediately?"

"Well, we haven't really had the chance to discuss it, but I can see the logic in that idea. Without a full translation of the cipher, the notebook would be considerably less useful. At the very least, I might suggest waiting until Xezia and Argus finish the translation, and then take that copy. I've already laid a logical groundwork for staying with the party, so I can continue as back-up for now."

Shar nodded. "I'll be meeting with Allistair in a week's time. Perhaps you could give us an update in five or six days." She pulled a pair of scrolls out of a desk drawer and muttered an incantation over them. Then she handed one of them to Xezia. "You know how these work, yes? Just write your update on this scroll, and when you sign it, what you wrote will disappear and appear on ours. Check yours a day later for a response."

"How many messages can we send?" he asked.

"Just two each way. Presumably you won't need more than that?"

"I certainly hope not," Sora answered.

"Is there anything else you might need from us?" Shar asked.

"Perhaps the locations of a couple of safe-houses in divergent directions," Daijera replied. "If we end up having to part ways in a hurry, we might need somewhere to go."

"Very prudent." Shar pulled out a small map of central Rosend. "There is a remote cottage here," she said, pointing to a spot very near Rosend's far western border, "just outside the Deep Woods. It's not fancy, but it is fairly well-provisioned if you need to lie low for a little while. There is also a blacksmith's shop in Galantus known as the Happy Horseshoe. The smith is one of us, and can give you a safe place to hide out for a couple of days. You can take the map with you."

"That should get us started," Xezia nodded. "Surely we can check in with a contact somewhere if we're about to find ourselves out of communication for a while."

Daijera raised an eyebrow at that. The mission seemed fairly straightforward, but Xezia was hedging. *Why?*

Shar noticed the hesitation, too, but seemed to dismiss it. "Feel free to enjoy our hospitality for a little while if you wish before returning to your inn. We have a few games of chance in the room at the end of the hall, as well as some fine food and libations."

"I believe we'll head back," Xezia decided, and Sora nodded. "Daijera, will you give us maybe twenty minutes before you leave?"

"Certainly. I'll see you in the morning. If I heard Argus correctly, we'll be leaving the inn a couple of hours after dawn, so we can get a little extra rest for a change."

Xezia nodded curtly to Daijera and Shar, and then he and Sora left the office.

Shar leaned in. "Does it seem to you like he's up to something?"

"It's possible. If I've learned anything about that man in the past week, it's that he's always thinking three moves ahead. I'm not sure that's any danger to the mission, though. He operates like anyone interested in climbing the Black Moon ladder."

That brought a hearty guffaw from Shar. "You know, I hadn't thought of it that way, but you're exactly right. He reminds me of a younger Allistair, though this one is a bit more sullen. Got an awful lot of darkness around him for an Epi mage, don't you think?"

It felt to Daijera like Shar was fishing for information, and she was overplaying her hand. Did Allistair have doubts about Xezia's loyalty or intentions? If those doubts grew too great, that generally only ended one way ... with Xezia's not-so-mysterious disappearance. She had never met Allistair, and this was only the third time she'd met Shar.

In contrast, she'd spent the last week with Xezia and Sora, and felt like she was reading them pretty well. Reading people, after all, was one of her specialties. Was he up to something? Probably. Would he endanger the mission? Probably not directly; he was too smart for that. Should his loyalty be questioned? Not his loyalty to Sora, certainly, but it wasn't clear how far his other loyalties extended.

"I'd have to agree with that, Shar, but I don't think I'd draw a conclusion as to the cause. If he's chosen to follow Epi, I suspect his darkness is related to something other than a lust for power."

Shar considered this for a moment. "Keep an eye on him, Daijera. Remember that your first loyalty is to the organization, and second to that are the individual agents."

"I'm well aware. My loyalty and reputation are beyond reproach, or you wouldn't have asked Savita to put me in as back-up. I know it was you; Allistair doesn't even know me."

Shar laughed again. "You always were the clever one. I've never understood your lack of ambition. You could head up a cell somewhere if you put the time in."

"I don't want to run anything. I don't want responsibility for anything beyond my own hide and whatever mission I'm on. I like being friends with the powerful, but I don't want to BE powerful."

"All of the benefits, none of the work, eh?"

"Exactly. Which is why you know I can be trusted. I'm not after your job, or anyone else's. I gather intel, I make sure the right people know what they need to know. I take on some additional tasks when necessary. Then I go back to my very nice rooms with a view of the river where I have pretty clothes, good food, and don't have to watch my back."

"Clever, clever, clever," Shar laughed again. "Will you do us the honor of performing a couple of songs before you go? Maybe that number you did the night we met at Morshak House? When you did your illusion magic to create the fog when you sang about the moors?"

"I'd be honored to perform for your guests, Shar." Daijera gave her warmest smile. "I'd also be honored to sample some of your finest spirits."

"If you lived here in Swanford, I suspect we'd be marvelous friends."

"I do like powerful friends," she winked.

Argus

It was positively infuriating to have to wait so late in the morning before going to the library to see Aerith. If Argus had only known where she lived, there was no way he would have hesitated in going to see her the night before, when they first arrived in Swanford.

As it was, though, no one dawdled about in the morning, and they were all waiting outside the library doors when she arrived to unlock them. At the sight of Argus, she gasped and dropped the bag of books she had been carrying. She ran to him and grasped his hands in hers, her deep blue eyes shining with tears.

"Argus, thank the Six you've come." She was a tiny woman, with hair that had once been the color of fire, still somewhat visible among the wispy gray. It had the effect of making her head look like a cloudy sunrise. She was in her sixties, but as brilliant as she had been half as many years ago. "I was so lost in my studies that I didn't notice the bowls until three days ago. I sent a message to your tavern in case you hadn't seen ..."

"I had a feeling you might not see the portent right away, and I've been traveling back and forth from Zaos's tower for the past week. How stands his bowl today? Is he alive?"

"Let us go check. The liquid was still muddy last night." She unlocked the heavy wooden doors and began to lead everyone inside. "I see you have brought friends to help you search for Zaos?"

"After a fashion. Aerith Lin, this is Ren, Xezia, Sora, Ekko, Daijera, and Dalgis. Dalgis," he added quickly, "if you go round the back of the building, I'll open up the window to Aerith's office so you can be part of our conversation."

"Why, thank you, Argus. That is extraordinarily considerate of you. I shall meet you there." He trotted off, clearly pleased at being included.

Aerith watched him go. "What manner of beast is that?"

"Dalgis is a wizard's creation, if I understand his history correctly."

"You don't suppose he's something Yousef cooked up do you?" she almost whispered.

"You mean Yousef Gonestible? I'm afraid I don't know much about him. I know he lived in the southern plains of Ironshield, and that he was one of Godfroy's first casualties when he came into power. I remember hearing that he was burned as a heretic on account of his research. It was a great cautionary tale as I was apprenticing in Ironshield with the Wizards' Guild."

"Yes indeed. I knew Yousef. A fine man, but there were many who thought his magical experiments were inspired by Rahmgn himself. There was little rhyme or reason to his research; he just asked 'what if…' and off he went wherever the path led."

Aerith approached her office door and reached in her pocket for another key. She began patting her robes frantically, searching other pockets, and finding nothing.

"I believe this is yours, good lady," Ren held out the bag she had dropped in the street, and she was visibly relieved.

"Oh, thank you, young man. Yes, I'm sure the key is there." She took the bag from him and fished around, eventually coming up with a small silver key. She tapped it to the lock three times, and the door popped open. Argus shook his head in amusement.

They stepped inside her office and looked immediately at the shelf of glass bowls displayed behind her desk, just as it was behind Argus's, Kieran's, and Zaos's. There was no change in the colors of the liquid, and Argus let out a breath. He closed his eyes for a moment, then went to the window to let Dalgis in, at least from the neck up.

"Aerith, I think there is something you need to know. I said that these folks," he waved over at the party, "were somewhat joining me to help look for Zaos, but it's a bit more complicated than that. Before he was abducted, Zaos hired this group to take his research notes to Kieran …"

"Oh, skies above us! He would never have parted with his life's work! He must have known he was in dire peril!" She crossed her hands over her chest as though she were counting heartbeats.

"Exactly our thought. But there is more to it …"

"Oh, no, and Kieran is dead! What is happening?"

"Breathe, Aerith, and let me finish the story. These people arrived at Kieran's with the journal as agreed, but Kieran was gone, and his house was ransacked."

"Ransacked! Was he …"

"Yes, ransacked," Argus interrupted, well aware that if he didn't get the story out, Aerith might go off on a tangent and he'd never get to tell her the whole thing. "They proceeded to look for clues as to what might have happened, and that was when I arrived. I had left Breadstone several days earlier, you see, having noticed the bowls …"

"Oh, I see …"

"And then we all traveled together back to Zaos's tower to return his research to him, and sadly, we found Kieran's body on the way. We gave him a burial, then proceeded to Zaos's tower, only to find that his home had been tossed as well, and that a travel spell had been cast. I was rather hoping to find him here with you, but I see that is not what happened." Argus took a breath, having caught her up on the basics.

"So, you have the journal, then?"

"We do," he replied, "and it was encoded. We've been working on the decryption ..."

"Are you sure that's wise?" Aerith's eyes darted ever-so-briefly to the party.

"If I may," interjected Xezia, "we felt, and Argus agreed, that it was important to know what Zaos was protecting. Argus tells us, and I assume you already know this, that Ironshield is looking to possess the Divine Books. If Godfroy gets his hands on any of their power, that spells bad news for the rest of the kingdoms. We needed to know if this was, indeed, as valuable as everyone thinks it is."

Aerith narrowed her eyes at Xezia, clearly feeling he was overstepping his bounds. "And was it?" she asked, somewhat testily.

"It was," chimed in Sora.

"Aerith," Argus stepped in, hoping she would listen if it was him saying it, "we all agree that we should pursue Utrui's book. If Godfroy has taken Zaos ..." He paused to clear his throat, not wanting to think about what Godfroy and his zealots would do to the elderly wizard to get information. "I know Zaos would never give them information willingly, but you know as well as I do that there are ways, both magical and non-magical, to get someone to talk, no matter how strong their mind may be. My friend, we'd like to leave Zaos's journal here with you, and if Ironshield comes for it, give it to them. Don't risk your life. We'll take the cipher key with us, so it will take anyone who acquires the journal a great deal of time to translate it, and that should slow them down. We have to get the Book of Order before that lunatic does."

"I don't like this, Argus. No offense to all of you," she said, sincerely apologetic, "but none of you have taken the oaths we have. I'd like to think you are all honorable people, but ..."

"We're not," Daijera confessed. "Most of us were in it for the money, at least at the beginning. But none of us want to see what will happen if the Blood King gains divine magic, assuming that's even what the Books are. We must keep it out of his hands at all costs."

Argus surveyed Daijera with the beginnings of appreciation. He still didn't like her much, and he was pretty sure he didn't trust her, no matter what her aura said, but her words were impassioned and persuasive.

"Here, here!" Dalgis cried, clearly excited that new adventures loomed on the horizon.

Aerith looked over the group, then back to Argus. "Very well, then, Argus. I trust your judgement. Give me an hour to pack and we'll be off."

"What? Aerith, you can't be serious. You're near seventy. This is a very arduous journey."

"It is, but you need my assistance. I worked with Zaos on that research, and I don't need a cipher key to know where to look for Utrui's Book. This was my life's work, just as it was his. Besides, you are a strong and powerful man, but I have stronger magic than yours and the twenty-five extra years I have on you also mean twenty-five years of experience and knowledge. This will likely be as much a battle of wits as it will be a test of strength and endurance."

Argus opened his mouth to argue, but he knew that she was right. She was like a living version of the journal, and her wisdom would be invaluable and save them a great deal of time. There was also the strong probability that Ironshield would come for her next, and at least this way, he could protect her.

"All right, everyone," he sighed, "let's do what we must to provision ourselves for the journey. We meet back here in about an hour, and then we head out to get the Book before Godfroy does."

"Huzzah!" cheered Dalgis.

Itching to see what happens next?

Check out the preview of

IRONSHIELD'S SHADOW: *THE BOOK OF ORDER*

at the end of this volume.

Chapter Nine

Preview of The Book of Order

Chapter 1: Into the Darkness

Elia

Walking all the way to the sea had been a stupid idea, Elia realized.

It had been nothing more than the illusion of a plan, a way to console herself that she was making forward progress. But as the days dragged on, she realized more and more clearly how she hadn't thought through the practical implications of this idea.

Problem one: She didn't know how to hunt. She was pretty sure she could recognize two or three berries that were safe to eat, but other than that, she also didn't know how to forage. It wasn't a skill she had ever had an opportunity to learn; she had lived in a fair-sized town all her life. So with the exception of a little bit of hard tack she'd found in one of the bags she scavenged, Elia had nothing to eat.

Problem two: She had to keep to the forest because if she was seen on a road, it could only go badly. Citizens of Heavenly Skies would (rightly) assume that she was from Ironshield, and if she should run into an Ironshield patrol, the best case scenario involved her being dragged back into a war she hated. Worst case scenario included her being recognized and declared AWOL, and brought back as a traitor. There would be no hearing, she'd be executed as an example to others who were considering desertion.

Problem three (closely related to problem two): She didn't have the right equipment for traversing heavy underbrush. That made going extremely slow and strenuous, which was exhausting, and fed back into problem one.

She had no idea how far she'd actually traveled, and it had been two days since she'd eaten anything. So when the smell of cooking meat hit her nostrils, she nearly fell to her knees. She cursed her human nose and its inability to track an exact direction for the delicious aroma.

Elia tried to follow the smell, but the shifting winds tricked her more than once, and she ended up backtracking and starting the search over. Finally, she heard the crackling sounds of a small fire in the distance, betraying the location she sought. Her nose might have failed her, but her ears came through. She made her way almost desperately toward the fire.

"Come, child. I have been waiting for you," came a slightly nasal voice ahead of her. She froze, sensing danger. "No need to be afraid. I have been sent to you as a blessing."

The smell of the meat overcame her better sense, at least partially. She began to move toward the voice. "A blessing from whom?"

"Just a blessing. Come and eat. You must be starving. And then we shall talk."

She saw a small clearing up ahead, aglow with firelight. A figure sat by the fire in a hooded cloak, its entire appearance hidden from view except for delicate hands of a smoky gray color which reached out from the folds of the robe and turned a skinned rabbit on a spit over the fire. Elia approached from the figure's right, but it never looked up to watch her approach.

"Who are you?" she asked.

"I am Syl. I come to offer you food and counsel, young one."

"How could you possibly have known where I would be? Even I don't know where I am."

A mirthless chuckle emanated from the figure. "Your coming was foretold to me. You are exactly where you are supposed to be, which in this case is the middle of nowhere."

"What does that even mean?"

Syl removed the rabbit from the fire and deftly cut off a chunk of meat with a bejeweled dagger, then extended it toward Elia. "Why don't you eat before we talk?"

Something inside her told her that it was unwise to take food from a creepy stranger, but the hunger gnawing at her gut didn't care what that little voice said. She plucked the hunk of meat off the dagger, blew on it just a little, and then shoved it into her mouth. She sighed as the slightly greasy juices ran over her tongue. She chewed and swallowed much faster than was polite.

Syl pulled a wooden bowl from a bag, and dropped the remainder of the rabbit into it. "Why don't you finish it?

You seem famished." The gray hand held the bowl out to Elia, and she took it without hesitation. If Syl was trying to poison her, then she was already doomed, so she might as well die full.

She tried to maintain some semblance of manners as she devoured the rabbit, and only when she'd picked the carcass clean did she realize she should have stopped eating halfway through and offered the remainder to her host.

"I'm so sorry. That was so rude. I ate the entire thing."

"Never apologize for ensuring that your own needs are met. Now then, shall we have a chat?" Syl reached up and dropped back the hood, and Elia couldn't help but gasp. The face looking back at her was like none she'd ever seen. Syl's face was the same color gray as the hands that had so expertly cooked the meat, so that part wasn't shocking. What took Elia aback was the complete lack of features on Syl's face. There were eyes, but they were the same shadowy gray, and the nose and eyes were nothing more than darker lines in the shadow.

The line that was Syl's mouth bent upwards at the corners. Clearly, the intent had been to elicit a reaction.

"What are ... wait ... are you a changeling?" Elia had heard stories of such creatures, faceless shifters that could become anyone or anything they touched, as long as they remained roughly the same size. Most of the stories she had heard involved changelings stealing human children to sacrifice to their dark gods, then taking the child's place and pretending to grow up, terrorizing the family for years.

"I am an *auf*, indeed. You should feel greatly honored that I show you my natural form."

"Is it true that you can become anyone you've touched?" Elia was simultaneously revulsed and fascinated.

"It is." Syl's skin began to pulse and move as it began to shift. Its skin warmed to a peachy color, and short black hair sprouted from its head. Its round gray eyes stretched into an almond shape and the irises darkened to almost black. Elia found herself staring at a young man of maybe nineteen who wouldn't have looked out of place in any of Ironshield's markets.

"Whoa," was all she could think to say.

The now-human face smiled. "You've had quite a journey the last couple of days."

"How do you know that?"

"I am a mage with the gift of prophecy. I know a great many things. Like I know that you are at a great crossroads in your life, and you are charging forward foolishly, without considering options or consequences."

"Say that's true. What difference does that make to you?" she asked.

"To me personally, not much, but to the one I represent? It makes a great deal of difference. You seem to have a rebellious streak and a strong spirit. These are great tools for building a future."

"What future?"

"Why, any one you wish, of course."

"This doesn't make any sense. I'm sorry if I'm being offensive, Syl. I do appreciate the food. But something feels amiss here."

"Things feel amiss wherever I go," Syl smiled. "But perhaps I should give you a little more concrete advice. You should return to Ironshield at once."

"Why would I do that?"

"Because Ironshield needs rabble-rousers like yourself right now. Godfroy has had his day; his time will run out soon enough. This war of his is unpopular, no matter what he thinks. Now is the time to sow the seeds of discontent, not to run away."

"I don't want to sow any seeds. I want to live a quiet, anonymous life somewhere."

"Ah, but do you really? Haven't you always had a talent for making your will a reality?"

"I guess so, but now my will is taking me out of here. Very far out of here."

Syl shifted back to its shadowy form. "Is it? Best be on your way then."

Warning bells were ringing in Elia's head. She needed to get away from this creature, NOW. "Uh, well, yes, I guess so. Thank you for the food. Perhaps we'll meet again."

"I have no doubt, young one."

Elia backed out of the clearing and tried her best to orient herself to the west. At night, it was a little hard to tell direction, and she didn't know how to navigate by the stars. After walking for a few minutes, she saw a light up ahead in the trees. She slowed down and approached carefully and quietly.

When she reached the source of the light, she broke into a cold sweat.

There sat Syl, tending its fire, chuckling its hollow chuckle.

Elia backed away and skirted around the clearing to the north, she thought, but in a few hundred yards, she found herself staring at the same clearing with the same creepy changeling tending the same sputtering fire.

She tried again, in a random direction this time, but it was only a minute or two before she found herself in Syl's clearing again. "What is happening?" she asked the auf.

"I'm helping you make the right choice," came the reply.

"Well, stop it! I do what I want!"

"Do you now?"

Over and over, she fled the clearing, and over and over, she found herself facing the faceless being. She felt as though she was losing her grip on her sanity.

"I refuse! I refuse!" she screamed and pulled out her dagger. "No one controls me!" She turned the dagger toward her heart, but before she could plunge the blade into her breast, there was a howl and a blinding light, and then all was empty.

Want more?

IRONSHIELD'S SHADOW: *The Book of Order* continues the quest!

Chapter Ten

Character Guide

The Deities of the Realm

Epi (Ep'-ee): Deity of Purity

Hohn (Hōn): Deity of Life

Hoshkn (Hōsh'-kĭn): Deity of Death

Ipthel (Ĭp'-thəl): Deity of Corruption

Utrui (Oo-troo'-ee): Deity of Order

Rahmgn (Rahm'-ghĭn): Deity of Chaos

The Adventurers

Argus (Ar'-gəs): Human. A wizard and one of the renowned Scholars of the Six, who resides and runs a tavern in Breadstone, in the north of Ironshield.

Daijera (Dī-jeer'-ə): Lamia. Resides in Nightveil, on the coast of Heavenly Skies. An agent of the Black Moon skilled at information brokering and the occasional assassination. By trade, a storyteller and musician.

Dalgis (Dahl'-ghĭs): Unique and un-named species, but dubbed a "pheonix lizard" by a child from Wheatfields. Nomadic, but originated in southwestern Ironshield. Was magically created by his "father", Yousef Gonestible, who was executed by King Godfroy for his magical/biological experiments.

Ekko (Ĕk'-ō): Werefox. Nomadic, but originally from central Rosend. A skilled young thief who has been living off of her wits since she was 12.

Elia (Ĕl'-lee-ə): Human. Orphaned as a child and raised by her Aunt Mita in Breadstone, in northern Ironshield. Trained as an herbalist before being conscripted into King Godfroy's army.

Ren (Rehn'): Human. Originally from northern Rosend, but raised in Davit, outside of Ironshield City. Trained to be a knight to the royal Talon family before the usurpation by King Godfroy.

Xezia (Zā'-zee-ə): Mixed race of sun elf, human, and orc. Mage of Epi. Ambitious agent of Black Moon, interested in rising to a position of power, ostensibly to bend the organization to less corrupt ways. Originally from a (now destroyed) village in eastern Heavenly Skies.

Sora (Sōr'-ə): Sun elf. Smuggler working for Black Moon who owes Xezia a blood debt, and thus must stay by his side until released from her vow. Raised in the town of Halasa in Benedictus.

Met Along the Way

Allistair: Regional leader of the Black Moon. Assigned Daijera, Sora, and Xezia to take possession of Zaos's journal.

Jasah: A small half-elf, half-dryad child living in Wheatfields. Assigns Dalgis the breed name of *phoenix lizard*.

Kieran: One of the Scholars of the Six. Lives in Wheatfields in Rosend and has possession of the cipher key for Zaos's notes.

Shar: Regional lieutenant of Allistair's within the Black Moon. She operates out of a hidden headquarters in Swanford.

Zaos: A wizard and mage of Utrui, the God of Order, and one of the Scholars of the Six. Zaos has devoted his life to studying the truth behind the folklore surrounding the six Deities, Utrui in particular. Zaos believes he has narrowed down the location of the Book of Order, a divine book thought widely to be a myth.

CHAPTER ELEVEN

ABOUT THE CO-CREATORS

Always pondering their next creative venture, **Lea Scism** is the type of person whose head would explode without a project to work on. Their journals are filled with stories and drawings about all manner of fantastical beings, from the wonderful to the horrifying. Previously shared only among friends, with the aid of like-minded writers like JB Caine and Sam Hamilton, they're now working on putting all that imagination before a wider audience.

Sam Hamilton has never been a writer. But D&D gave them a chance to create stories in a way that felt more obtainable. They found a love for playing D&D in high school with their friends and my first campaign and discovered a love of lore and side quests. Years later, they finally felt comfortable co-running a game with the amazing world-builder Lea Scism for the Speech & Debate team, and together they created a story that helped them fall in love with the game even more. With the talents of JB Caine, that game has come to life...a reality they never expected. They are so excited for the future as a player and as a DM.

www.ingramcontent.com/pod-product-compliance
Lightning Source LLC
Chambersburg PA
CBHW060755310726
48980CB00002B/107

* 9 7 9 8 9 9 9 0 7 9 9 7 8 *